The Cube Root of Uncertainty

The Cube Root of
Uncertainty

Robert Silverberg

THE MACMILLAN COMPANY

The Macmillan Company
866 Third Avenue, New York, N.Y. 10022
Collier-Macmillan Canada Ltd., Toronto, Ontario

Library of Congress Catalog Card Number: 70-107051

FIRST PRINTING
Printed in the United States of America

ACKNOWLEDGMENTS

"Passengers," Copyright © 1968 by Damon Knight. Reprinted from *Orbit*.

"Double Dare," Copyright © 1956 by Galaxy Publishing Corporation. Reprinted from *Galaxy*.

"The Sixth Palace," Copyright © 1965 by Galaxy Publishing Corporation. Reprinted from *Galaxy*.

"Translation Error," Copyright © 1959 by Street & Smith Publications, Inc. Reprinted from *Astounding Science Fiction*.

"The Shadow of Wings," Copyright © 1963 by Galaxy Publishing Corporation. Reprinted from *If*.

"Absolutely Inflexible," Copyright © 1956 by King-Size Publications, Inc. Reprinted from *Fantastic Universe*.

"The Iron Chancellor," Copyright © 1958 by Galaxy Publishing Corporation. Reprinted from *Galaxy*.

"Mugwump Four," Copyright © 1959 by Galaxy Publishing Corporation. Reprinted from *Galaxy*.

"To the Dark Star," Copyright © 1968 by Joseph Elder. Reprinted from *The Farthest Reaches*.

"Neighbor," Copyright © 1964 by Galaxy Publishing Corporation. Reprinted from *Galaxy*.

"Halfway House," Copyright © 1966 by Galaxy Publishing Corporation. Reprinted from *If*.

"Sundance," Copyright © 1969 by Mercury Publications, Inc. Reprinted from *Fantasy & Science Fiction*.

For Harry Harrison
who signed the first check

Contents

Introduction

THE UNIVERSE is full of pitfalls and trap doors. Some of us find that out very early; others don't learn it for a while, but in time the news gets to all of us. I'm not referring to the final trap door through which we all must drop, for the only surprises in that lie in the timing and manner of the exit. I mean the nasty little calamities that strew the path between cradle and grave—the unexpected, unwanted, unhappy things coming out of nowhere. Call it the will of God, call it the law of averages; the effect is the same. Plato warns us to speak of no man as happy until his life has ended, since even the happiest of mortals may come upon dark times before his course is run. Just so.

It takes very little imagination to suggest a dozen ways in which our lives can be boobytrapped. The newspapers teem with the horrors that smite us: the swerving auto, the collapsing bridge, the ptomaine in the vichyssoise, the fishhook in the filet of sole. Air conditioners plummet from apartment-house windows; jet engines drop from passing airliners; choirboys climb bell towers to spray the street with bullets. Our wonder drugs turn out to have mysterious side effects, our television sets are found to emanate hard radiation, our automobiles seem to disassemble themselves at critical moments. Our lives may intersect nightmare at any moment.

Many of these potential calamities are quite new; no one in the nineteenth century was ever menaced by thalidomide, a defective automobile, or a falling airplane engine. As life grows ever more complex, the possibilities of calamity grow steadily more manifold, and more interesting as well, I think. (What about hallucinogenic drugs in the water supply? Atomic power plants in earthquake zones? The shock-wave damage done by a crashing spaceship?) And the job of the science fiction writer is to look beyond tomorrow, seeking newer and stranger species of chaos.

One great virtue of science fiction is that it can simultaneously transmute nightmare into entertainment and entertainment into nightmare. The science fiction writer specializes in dropping his characters through trap doors —trap doors that have not yet been invented. To meet yourself on a time trip, to have your household dominated by a dictatorial robot, to take up orbit around a dying star, to submit to the whims of invisible and omnipotent conquerors of our planet—these are experiences reserved, thank heaven, for our descendants. But we can sample them vicariously via science fiction, and derive the consolation of knowing that if life seems tricky and uncertain now, it's going to be uncertainty cubed in centuries to come.

The stories in this collection were written between 1954 and 1968. The lean young man responsible for the earliest ones lived in a bygone era when spaceflight was an opium dream, television came in black and white, and airplanes had propellers. The author of the bleak and thorny stories with the most recent copyright dates has had fifteen more years of exposure to the trap doors of the universe than his youthful counterpart, and has found it an instructive if not always delightful experience. The progression from such cheery tales as "Double Dare" and "Mugwump Four" to such grim ones as "Passengers" and "Sundance" may indicate to the perceptive reader that my outlook on our treacherous universe has grown no brighter with time. But the warning is clear: the gorgeous worst is yet to come.

—ROBERT SILVERBERG

The Cube Root of Uncertainty

Passengers

$\cdots\!\!-\!\!\!\!-\!\!\!\!\circledcirc\!\!-\!\!\!\!-\!\!\cdots$

THERE ARE only fragments of me left, now. Chunks of memory have broken free and drifted away like calved glaciers. It is always like that when a Passenger leaves us. We can never be sure of all the things our borrowed bodies did. We have only the lingering traces, the imprint.

Like sand clinging to an ocean-tossed bottle. Like the throbbings of amputated legs.

I rise. I collect myself. My hair is rumpled; I comb it. My face is creased from too little sleep. There is sourness in my mouth. Has my Passenger been eating dung with my lips? They do that. They do anything.

It is morning.

A gray, uncertain morning. I stare at it a while, and then, shuddering, I opaque the window and confront instead the gray, uncertain surface of the inner panel. My room looks untidy. Did I have a woman here? There are ashes in the trays. Searching for butts, I find several with lipstick stains. Yes, a woman was here.

I touch the bedsheets. Still warm with shared warmth. Both pillows tousled. She has gone, though, and the Passenger is gone, and I am alone.

How long did it last, this time?

I pick up the phone and ring Central. "What is the date?" I ask.

The computer's bland feminine voice replies, "Friday, December four, 1987."

"The time?"

"Nine fifty-one, Eastern Standard Time."

"The weather forecast?"

"Predicted temperature range for today, thirty to thirty-eight. Current temperature, thirty-one. Wind from the north, sixteen miles an hour. Chances of precipitation slight."

"What do you recommend for a hangover?"

"Food or medication?"

"Anything you like," I say.

The computer mulls that one for a while. Then it decides on both, and activates my kitchen. The spigot yields cold tomato juice. Eggs begin to fry. From the medicine slot comes a purplish liquid. The Central Computer is always so thoughtful. Do the Passengers ever ride it, I wonder? What thrills could that hold for them? Surely it must be more exciting to borrow the million minds of Central than to live a while in the faulty, short-circuited soul of a corroding human being!

December 4, Central said. Friday. So the Passenger had me for three nights.

I drink the purplish stuff and probe my memories in a gingerly way, as one might probe a festering sore.

I remember Tuesday morning. A bad time at work. None of the charts will come out right. The section manager irritable; he has been taken by Passengers three times in five weeks, and his section is in disarray as a result, and his Christmas bonus is jeopardized. Even though it is customary not to penalize a person for lapses due to Passengers, according to the system. The section manager seems to feel he will be treated unfairly. So he treats us unfairly. We have a hard time. Revise the charts, fiddle with the program, check the fundamentals ten times over. Out they come: the detailed forecasts for price variations of public utility securities, February–April, 1988. That afternoon we are to meet and discuss the charts and what they tell us.

I do not remember Tuesday afternoon.

That must have been when the Passenger took me. Perhaps at work; perhaps in the mahogany-paneled board room itself, during the conference. Pink concerned faces all about me; I cough, I lurch, I stumble from my seat. They shake their heads sadly. No one reaches for me. No one stops me. It is too dangerous to interfere with one who has a Passenger. The chances are great that a second Passenger lurks nearby in the discorporate state, looking for a mount. So I am avoided. I leave the building.

After that, what?

Sitting in my room one bleak Friday morning, I eat my scrambled eggs and try to reconstruct the three lost nights.

Of course it is impossible. The conscious mind functions during the period of captivity, but upon withdrawal of the Passenger nearly every recollection goes too. There is only a slight residue, a gritty film of faint and ghostly memories. The mount is never precisely the same person afterwards; though he cannot recall the details of his experience, he is subtly changed by the essence of it.

I try to recall.

A girl? Yes: lipstick on the butts. Sex, then, here in my room. Young? Old? Blonde? Dark? Everything is hazy. How did my borrowed body behave? Was I a good lover? I try to be, when I am myself. I keep in shape. At thirty-eight, I can handle three sets of tennis on a summer afternoon without collapsing. I can make a woman glow as a woman is meant to glow. Not boasting: just categorizing. We have our skills. This is mine.

But Passengers, I am told, take wry amusement in controverting our skills. So would it have given my rider a kind of delight to find me a woman and force me to fail repeatedly with her?

I dislike that thought. I shove it away.

The fog is going from my mind now. The medicine prescribed by Central works rapidly. I eat, I shave, I stand under the vibrator until my skin is clean. I do my exercises. Did the Passenger exercise my body Wednesday and Thursday mornings? Probably not. I must make up for that. I am close to middle age, now; tonus lost is not easily regained.

I touch my toes twenty times, knees stiff.

I kick my legs in the air.

I lie flat and lift myself on pumping elbows.

The body responds, maltreated though it has been. It is the first bright moment of my awakening: to feel the inner tingling, to know that I still have vigor. The stain of being ridden is ebbing from me.

Fresh air is what I want next. Quickly I slip into my clothes and leave my room. There is no need for me to report to work today. They are aware that since Tuesday afternoon I have had a Passenger; they need not be aware that before dawn of Friday the Passenger departed. In some ways there are advantages to this dreadful thing that has befallen our world. I will have a free day. I will walk the city's streets, stretching my limbs, repaying my body for the abuse it has suffered.

I enter the elevator. I drop fifty stories to the ground. I step out into the December dreariness.

The towers of New York rise about me.

In the street the cars stream forward. Drivers sit edgily at their wheels. One never knows when the driver of a nearby car will be borrowed, and there is always a moment of lapsed coordination as the Passenger takes over. Many lives are lost that way on our streets and highways; but never the life of a Passenger.

I begin to walk without purpose. I cross 14th Street, heading north, listening to the soft violet purr of the electric engines. I see a boy jigging in the street and know he is being ridden. At Fifth and 22nd a prosperous-looking paunchy man approaches, his necktie askew, this morning's *Wall Street Journal* jutting from an overcoat pocket. He giggles. He thrusts out his tongue. Ridden. Ridden. I avoid him. Moving briskly, I come to the underpass that carries traffic below 34th Street toward Queens, and pause for a moment to watch two adolescent girls quarreling at the rim of the pedestrian walk. One is a Negro. Her eyes are rolling in terror. The other pushes her closer to the railing. Ridden. But the Passenger does not have murder on its mind, merely pleasure. The Negro girl is released and falls in a huddled heap, trembling. Then she rises and runs. The other girl draws a long blonde strand of gleaming hair into her mouth, chews on it, seems to awaken. She looks dazed.

I avert my eyes. One does not watch while a fellow sufferer is awakening. There is a morality of the ridden; we have so many new tribal mores in these dark days.

I hurry on.

Where am I going so hurriedly? Already I have walked more than a mile. I seem to be moving toward some predestined goal, as though my Passenger still hunches in my skull, urging me about. But I know that that is not so. For the moment, at least, I am free.

Can I be sure of that?

Cogito ergo sum no longer works. We go on thinking even while we are ridden, and we live in quiet desperation, unable to halt our courses no matter how ghastly, no matter how self-destructive. I am certain that I can distinguish between the condition of bearing a Passenger and the condition of being free. But perhaps not. Perhaps I bear a particularly devilish Passenger which has not quitted me at all, but which merely has receded to the cerebellum, leaving me the illusion of freedom while all the time surreptitiously driving me onward to some purpose of its own.

Did we ever have more than that: the illusion of freedom?

But this is disturbing, the thought that I may be ridden without realizing it. I burst out in heavy perspiration, not merely from the exertion of walking. Stop. Stop here. Why must you walk? You are at 42nd Street. There is the library. Nothing forces you onward. Stop a while, I tell myself. Rest on the library steps.

I sit on the cold stone and tell myself that I have made this decision for myself.

Have I? It is the old problem, free will vs. determinism, translated into the foulest of forms. Determinism is no longer a philosopher's abstraction; it is cold alien tendrils sliding between the cranial sutures. The Passengers arrived three years ago. I have been ridden five times since then. Our world is quite different now from the world I remember. But we have adjusted even to this. We have adjusted. We have our mores. Life goes on. Our governments rule, our legislatures meet, our stock exchanges transact business as usual, and we have methods for compensating for the random havoc. It is the only way. What else can we do? Shrivel in defeat? We have an enemy we cannot fight; at best we can resist through endurance. So we endure.

The stone steps are cold against my body. In December few people sit here.

I tell myself that I made this long walk of my own free will, that I halted of my own free will, that no Passenger bestrides my brain now. Perhaps. Perhaps. I cannot let myself believe that I may not be free. There must be intervals of freedom between the captivities.

Can it be, I wonder, that the Passenger left some lingering command in me? Walk to this place, halt at this place? That is possible, too. Not an agreeable thought, but preferable to the previous one.

I look about me at the others on the library steps.

An old man, eyes vacant, sitting on newspaper. A boy of thirteen or so with flaring nostrils. A plump woman. Are all of them ridden? Passengers seem to cluster about me today. The more I study the ridden ones, the more convinced I become that I am, for the moment, free. The last time, I had three months of freedom between rides. Some people, they say, are scarcely ever free. Their bodies are in great demand, and they know only scattered bursts of freedom, a day here, a week there, even an hour. We have never been able to determine how many Passengers infest our world. Millions, maybe. Or maybe five. Who can tell?

A wisp of snow curls down out of the gray sky. Central

had said the chance of precipitation was slight. Are they riding Central this morning too?

I see the girl.

She sits diagonally across from me, five steps up and a hundred feet away, her black shirt pulled up on her knees to reveal handsome legs. From this angle it reveals somewhat more than her calves and knees, too. She is young. Her hair is deep, rich auburn. Her eyes are pale; at this distance, I cannot make out the precise color. She is dressed simply. She is younger than thirty. She wears a dark green coat and her lipstick has a purplish tinge. Her lips are full, her nose slender, high-bridged, her eyebrows carefully plucked.

I know her.

I have spent the past three nights with her in my room. She is the one. Ridden, she came to me, and ridden, I slept with her. I am certain of this. The veil of memory parts; I see her slim body naked on my bed, the rosy-tipped breasts heaving, the arm outstretched, the birthmark above her rib.

How can it be that I remember this?

It is too strong to be an illusion. Clearly this is something that I have been *permitted* to remember, for reasons I cannot comprehend. And I remember more. I remember her soft gasping sounds of pleasure. I remember the texture of her skin. I remember her body throbbing in my arms. I know that my own body did not betray me those three nights, nor did I fail her need.

And there is more. A memory of sinuous music; a scent of youth in her hair; the rustle of winter trees. Somehow she brings back to me a time before this had befallen the world, a time when I am young and girls are mysterious, a time of parties and dances and warmth and secrets, a time when words like *love* and *hope* have not yet become blackened and corroded. I do not know why. I cannot imagine why.

I am drawn to her now.

There is an etiquette about such things, too. It is in poor taste to approach someone whom you met while being ridden. Such an encounter gives you no privilege; a stranger remains a stranger, no matter what you and she may have done and said during your involuntary time together. All vows and pledges induced by a Passenger are canceled with the departure of the Passenger. It is the only way. We cannot be held responsible for our Passengers' deeds.

Yet I am drawn to her.

Why this violation of taboo? Why this raw breach of etiquette? I have never done this before. I have been scrupulous.

But I get to my feet and walk along the step on which I have been sitting, until I am just below her, and I look up, and automatically she folds her ankles together and angles her knees as if in awareness that her position is not a modest one. I know from that gesture that she is not ridden now. My eyes meet hers. Her eyes are hazy green. She is beautiful, and I rack my memory for more details of our passion. None are forthcoming.

I climb step by step until I stand before her.

"Hello," I say.

She gives me a neutral look. She does not seem to recognize me. Her eyes are veiled, as one's eyes often are just after the Passenger has gone. She purses her lips and appraises me in a distant way.

Shall I pursue her now?

We can begin a relationship with the slate clear, I tell

myself. But the slate is *not* clear, not for me. I have had her already, and I know it. I am taking unfair advantage by approaching her this way. I am committing an abomination, by our new standards.

"Hello," she replies coolly. "I don't think I know you."

"No. You don't. But I have the feeling you don't want to be alone just now. And I know I don't." I try to persuade her with my eyes that my motives are decent. "There's snow in the air," I say. "We can find a warmer place. I'd like to talk to you."

"About what?"

"Let's go elsewhere, and I'll tell you. I'm Charles Roth."

"Helen Martin."

She gets to her feet. She still has not cast aside her cool neutrality; she is suspicious, ill at ease. But at least she is willing to go with me. A good sign.

"Is it too early in the day for a drink?" I ask.

"I'm not sure. I hardly know what time it is."

"Before noon."

"Let's have a drink anyway," she says, and we both smile.

We go to a cocktail lounge across the street. Sitting face to face in the darkness, we sip drinks, daiquiri for her, bloody Mary for me. She relaxes a little. I ask myself what it is I want from her. The pleasure of her company, yes. Her company in bed? But I have already had that pleasure, three nights of it, though she does not know that. I want something more. Something more. What?

Her eyes are bloodshot. She has had little sleep these past three nights.

I say, "Was it very unpleasant for you?"

"What?"

"The Passenger."

A whiplash of reaction crosses her face. "How did you know I've had a Passenger?"

"I know."

"We aren't supposed to discuss such things."

"I'm broadminded," I tell her. "My Passenger left me some time during the night. I was ridden since Tuesday afternoon."

"Mine left me about two hours ago, I think." Her cheeks color. She is doing something daring, talking like this. "I was ridden since Monday night. This was my fifth time."

"Mine also."

We toy with our drinks. Rapport is growing, almost without the need of words. Our recent experiences with Passengers give us a point in common, although Helen does not realize how intimately we shared those experiences. With this girl I have already performed every known passionate act, I suspect, and possibly some unknown ones, and yet all that is lost to me except the knowledge that it occurred. I must begin anew. Should I risk it?

We talk. She is a designer of display windows. She has a small apartment several blocks from here. She lives alone. She asks me what I do. "Securities analyst," I tell her. She smiles. Her teeth are flawless. She tells me of the stock she once purchased. It went down, she says. We have a second round of drinks. I am positive, now, that this is the girl who was in my room while I was ridden.

A seed of hope grows in me. It was a happy chance that brought us together again, so soon after we parted as dreamers. A happy chance, too, that some vestige of the dream lingered in my mind.

I want to reach out to her, to gather her close.

We have shared something, who knows what, and it must have been good to leave such a vivid imprint on me, and now I want to come to her conscious, aware, my own master, and renew that relationship, making it a real one this time. It is not proper, for I am trespassing on a privilege that is not mine except by virtue of our Passengers' brief presence in us. Yet I need her. I want her.

She seems to need me, too, without realizing who I am. But fear holds her back.

I am frightened of frightening her, and I do not try to press my advantage too quickly. Perhaps she would take me to her apartment with her now, perhaps not, but I do not ask. We finish our drinks. We arrange to meet by the library steps again tomorrow. My hand momentarily brushes hers. Then she is gone.

I fill three ashtrays that night. Over and over I debate the wisdom of what I am doing. But why not leave her alone? I have no right to follow her. In the place our world has become, we are wisest to remain apart.

And yet—there is that stab of half-memory when I think of her. The blurred lights of lost chances behind the stairs, of girlish laughter in second-floor corridors, of stolen kisses, of tea and cake. I remember the girl with the orchid in her hair, and the one in the spangled dress, and the one with the child's face and the woman's eyes, all so long ago, all lost, all gone, and I tell myself that this one I will not lose, I will not permit her to be taken from me.

Morning comes, a quiet Saturday. I return to the library, hardly expecting to find her there, but she is there, on the steps, and the sight of her is like a reprieve. She looks wary, troubled; obviously she has done much thinking, little sleeping, this night past. Together we walk along Fifth Avenue. She is quite close to me, but she does not take my arm. Her steps are brisk, short, nervous.

I want to suggest that we go to her apartment instead of to the cocktail lounge. In these days we must move swiftly while we are free. But I know it would be a mistake to think of this relationship as a matter of tactics and logistics. Coarse haste would be fatal, bringing me perhaps an ordinary victory, a numbing defeat within it. In any even her mood hardly seems promising. I stare at her, thinking of string music and new snowfalls, and she looks toward the gray sky.

She says, "I can feel them watching me all the time. Like vultures swooping overhead, waiting, waiting. Ready to pounce."

"But there's a way of beating them. We can grab little scraps of life when they're not looking."

"They're *always* looking."

"No," I tell her. "There can't be enough of them for that. Sometimes they're looking the other way. And while they are, two people can come together and try to share warmth."

"But what's the use?"

"You're too pessimistic, Helen. They ignore us for months at a time. We have a chance. We have a chance."

But I cannot break through her shell of fear. She is paralyzed by the nearness of the Passengers, unwilling to begin anything out of the conviction that it will be snatched from her by our tormentors. We reach the building where she lives, and I hope she will relent and invite me in. For an instant she wavers, but only for an instant: she takes my hand in both of hers, and smiles, and the smile fades, and she is gone, leaving me only with the words, "Let's meet at the library again tomorrow. Noon."

I make the long chilling walk home alone.

Some of her pessimism seeps into me that night. It seems futile for us to try to salvage anything. More than that: wicked for me to seek her out, shameful to offer a hesitant love when I am not free. In this world, I tell myself, we should keep well clear of others, so that we do not harm anyone when we are seized and ridden.

I do not go to meet her in the morning.

It is best this way, I insist. I have no business trifling with her. I see her at the library, wondering why I am late, growing tense, impatient, then annoyed, at last leaving. She will be angry with me for breaking our date, but her anger will ebb, and she will forget me quickly enough. And I will try to forget her.

Monday comes. I return to work.

Naturally, no one discusses my absence with me. It is as though I have never been away. Quickly I learn what I have missed, and then I thumb the computer nodes and calculate what must be calculated. The market is strong that morning. The work is challenging; it is mid-morning before I think of Helen at all. But once I think of her, I can think of nothing else. My cowardice in standing her up. The childishness of Saturday night's dark thoughts. Why accept fate so passively? Why give in? I want to fight, now, to carve out a pocket of security despite the odds. I feel a deep conviction that it can be done. The Passengers may never bother the two of us again, after all. And that flickering smile of hers outside her building Saturday, that momentary glow—it should have told me that behind her wall of fear she felt the same hopes. She was waiting for me to lead the way. And I stayed home instead.

At lunchtime I go to the library, convinced it is futile.

But she is there. She paces along the steps; the wind slices at her slender figure. I go to her. I greet her.

She is silent a moment. "Hello," she says finally.

"I'm sorry about yesterday."

"I waited a long time for you."

I shrug. "I made up my mind that it was no use to come. But then I changed my mind again."

She tries to look angry. But her fury is a poor counterfeit, ringing hollow. I know she is pleased to see me again —else why did she come here today? She cannot hide her inner pleasure. Nor can I. I point across the street to the cocktail lounge.

"A daiquiri?" I say. "As a peace offering?"

"All right."

Today the lounge is crowded, but we find a booth somehow. There is a brightness in her eyes that I have not seen before. I sense that a barrier is crumbling within her.

"You're less afraid of me, Helen," I say.

"I've never been afraid of you. I'm afraid of what could happen if we take the risks."

"Don't be. Don't be."

"I'm trying not to be afraid. But sometimes it seems so hopeless. Since *they* came here—"

"We can still try to live our own lives."

"Maybe."

"We have to. Let's make a pact, Helen. No more gloom. No more worrying about the terrible things that might just maybe happen. All right?"

A pause. Then a cool hand against mine.

"All right."

We finish our drinks, and I present my Credit Central to pay for them, and we go outside. I want her to tell me to forget about this afternoon's work and come home with her. It is inevitable, now, that she will ask me, and better sooner than later.

We walk a block. She does not offer the invitation. I sense the struggle inside her, and I wait, letting that struggle reach its own resolution without interference from me. We walk a second block. Her arm is through mine, but she talks only of her work, of the weather, and it is a remote, arm's-length conversation. At the next corner she swings around, away from her apartment, back toward the cocktail lounge. I try to be patient with her.

I have no need to rush things now, I tell myself. Her body is not a secret to me. We have begun our relationship topsy-turvy, with the physical part first; now it will take time to work backward to the more difficult part that some people call love.

But of course she is not aware that we have known each other that way. The wind blows swirling snowflakes in our faces, and somehow the cold sting awakens honesty in me. I know what I must say. I must relinquish my unfair advantage.

I tell her, "While I was ridden last week, Helen, I had a girl in my room."

"Why talk of such things now?"

"I have to, Helen. You were the girl."

She halts. She turns to me. People hurry past us in the street. Her face is very pale, with dark red spots growing in her cheeks.

"That's not funny, Charles."

"It wasn't meant to be. You were with me from Tuesday night to early Friday morning."

"How can you possibly know that?"

"I do. I do. The memory is clear. Somehow it remains, Helen. I see your whole body."

"Stop it, Charles."

"We were very good together," I say. "We must have pleased our Passengers because we were so good. To see you again—it was like waking from a dream, and finding that the dream was real, the girl right there—"

"No!"

"Let's go to your apartment and begin again."

She says, "You're being deliberately filthy, and I don't know why, but there wasn't any reason for you to spoil things. Maybe I was with you and maybe I wasn't, but you wouldn't know it, and if you did know it you should keep your mouth shut about it the way any gentleman would, and—"

"You have a birthmark the size of a dime," I say, "about three inches below your left breast."

She sobs and hurls herself at me, there in the street. Her long silvery nails rake my cheeks and I feel the skin scraping away. She pummels me. I seize her. Her knees assail me. No one pays attention; those who pass by assume we are ridden, and turn their heads. She is all fury, but I have my arms around hers like metal bands, so that she can only stamp and snort, and her body is close against mine. She is rigid, anguished. Her heels punish my legs.

In a low, urgent voice I say, "We'll defeat them, Helen. We'll finish what they started. Don't fight me. There's no reason to fight me. I know, it's a fluke that I remember you, but let me go with you and I'll prove that we belong together."

"Let—go—"

"Please. Please. Why should we be enemies? I don't mean you any harm. I love you, Helen. Do you remember, when we were kids, we could play at being in love? I did; you must have done it, too. Sixteen, seventeen years old. The whispers, the conspiracies—all a big game, and we knew it. But the game's over. We can't afford to tease and run. We have so little time, when we're free—we have to trust, to open ourselves—"

"It's wrong."

"No. Just because it's the stupid custom for two people

brought together by Passengers to avoid one another, that doesn't mean we have to follow it. Helen—Helen—"

Something in my tone registers with her. She ceases to struggle. Her rigid body softens. She looks up at me, her tear-streaked face thawing, her eyes blurred.

"Trust me," I say. "Trust me, Helen!"

She hesitates. Then she nods.

She smiles.

In that moment I feel the chill at the back of my skull, the sensation as of a steel needle driven deep through bone. I stiffen. My arms drop away from her. For an instant, I lose touch, and when the mists clear all is different.

"Charles?" she says. "*Charles?*"

Her knuckles are against her teeth. I turn, ignoring her, and go back into the cocktail lounge. A young man sits in one of the front booths. His dark hair gleams with pomade; his cheeks are smooth. His eyes meet mine.

I sit down. He orders drinks. We do not talk.

My hand falls on his wrist, and it remains there. The bartender, serving the drinks, scowls but says nothing. We sip our cocktails and put the drained glasses down.

"Let's go," the young man says.

I follow him out.

Double Dare

•••—◄◉►—•••

B<small>Y THE TIME</small> the spaceship had finished jiggling and actually stood firmly on Domerangi soil, Justin Marner was beginning to doubt his sanity.

"We must be crazy," he said. "We *must* be."

The other Earthman, who had been gazing out the viewplate at the green-and-gold alien vista, glanced around suddenly at Marner's remark. "Huh?"

"There are limits to which one goes in proving a point," Marner said. He indicated the scene outside. "This little journey exceeds the limits. Now that we're here, Kemridge, I'm sure of it. *Nobody* does things like this."

Kemridge shrugged sourly. "Don't be silly Justin. You know why we're here, and you know how come we're here. This isn't any time to—"

"All right," Marner said. "I take it all back." He stared

for a moment at his delicate, tapering fingers—the fingers that could have belonged to a surgeon, were they not the property of a top-rank technical engineer. "Don't pay any attention to whatever I just said. It's the strain that's getting me."

The door of the cabin chimed melodiously.

"Come in," said Kemridge.

The door slid open and a Domerangi, clad in a bright yellow sash, gray-green buskins, and a glittering diadem of precious gems, stepped heavily into the cabin. He extended two of his five leathery tentacles in welcome.

"Hello, gentlemen. I see you've come through the trip in fine shape."

"What's going on now, Plorvash?" Marner asked.

"The ship has landed at a spaceport just outside the city," the alien said. "I've come to take you to your quarters. We're giving you two the finest accommodations our planet can offer. We want your working conditions to be of the best."

"Glad to hear it." Marner flicked a glance at his companion. "They're most considerate, aren't they, Dave?"

The taller of the two Earthmen nodded gravely. "Definitely."

Plorvash grinned. "Suppose you come with me now. You would like to be well rested before you undertake your task. After all, you should be at your best, since planetary pride is at stake."

"Of course," Marner said.

"The test will begin as soon as you wish. May I offer you good luck?"

"We won't need it," Kemridge stated grimly. "It's not a matter of luck at all. It's brains—brains and sweat."

"Very well," Plorvash said. "This is what you're here to prove. It ought to be amusing, in any case—whatever the outcome may be."

Both Earthmen tried to look calm and confident, absolutely sure of themselves and their skill.

They merely managed to look rigidly worried.

Statisticians have no records on the subject, but it is an observed phenomenon that the most serious differences of opinion generally originate in bars. It had been in a bar at 46th Street and Sixth Avenue that Justin Marner had ill-advisedly had words with a visiting Domerangi, a month before, and it had been in the same bar that the train of events that had brought the two Earthmen to Domerang V had started—and never stopped gaining momentum.

It had been a simple altercation at first. Marner had been reflectively sipping a whisky sour, and Kemridge, seated to his left with his long legs uncomfortably scrunched up, had been toying with a double Scotch. The Domerangi had entered the bar with a characteristically ponderous stride.

Though contact with Domerang V had been made more than a century before, Domerangi were still rare sights in New York. Marner and Kemridge knew this one, though —he was attached to the Domerangi Consulate on 66th Street and Third, and they had had dealings with him a year ago in the matter of some circuit alignments for the building's lighting system. Domerangi, with their extraordinary peripheral vision, prefer subdued, indirect lighting, and Marner and Kemridge had designed the lighting plot for the Consulate.

The Domerangi spotted them immediately and eased his bulk onto the stool next to them. "Ah, the two clever engineers," the alien rumbled. "You remember me, of course?"

"Yes," Marner said quickly. "How's the lighting job working out?"

"As well as could be expected." The Domerangi waved toward the bartender. "Barkeep! Two beers, please."

"What do you mean by that?" Kemridge demanded as the beers were drawn and set on the bar.

"Just one moment, please." The alien curled two tentacles gently around the beers and poured one into each of the two feeding-mouths at the sides of his face. "Marvelous liquid, your beer. The one point where Earth is clearly superior to Domerang is in brewing."

"To get back to the lights—" Kemridge prodded.

"Oh, yes," the alien said. "The lights. Well, they're a pretty fair job—as good as we could have hoped for from a second-rate technology."

"Now hold on a minute!" Marner said hotly, and that was how it started.

"I wish we'd kept our mouths shut," Marner said glumly. He stared balefully at the spotless ceiling of the hotel room in which the Domerangi had installed them.

Kemridge whirled and glared down at the smaller man. "Listen, Justin: we're here and we're going to show them up and go home rich and famous. Got that?"

"Okay," Marner said. He ran a finger along his thin lower lip. "I'm sorry I keep popping off like this. But it does seem screwy to have gone to this extent just to prove a point that came up in a barroom debate."

"I know. But we wouldn't have come here if the State Department hadn't heard about the argument and thought it needed settling. The Domerangi have been acting lordly about their technology as long as we've known them. I think it's a great idea to send a couple of honest-to-Christmas Terran engineers up here to show them once and for all who's got what it takes."

"But suppose we *don't* show them?"

"We will! Between the two of us, we can match anything they throw at us. Can't we?"

Marner smiled gloomily. "Sure we can," he said without conviction. "I haven't doubted it for one minute."

Kemridge walked to the door and, with a swift searching motion of his fingers, found the plate that covered the door mechanism. He unclipped it.

"Look in here, for example," he said, after a moment's scrutiny. "Simple cybernetic mechanism. I don't quite figure the way this green ceramic relay down here controls the power flow, but it's nothing we couldn't dope out, given a screwdriver and a little spare time."

Marner stood on tiptoes and peered in. "Perfectly understandable gadget," he commented. "Not nearly as efficient as our kind, either."

"That's just the point," Kemridge said. "These Domerangi aren't half the sharks they think they are. We stipulated that we could duplicate anything they gave us, right? With our natural savvy and a little perspiration, we ought to be able to match the best gadget they test us with. If we follow through up here and those two Domerangi engineers on Earth mess up their half of the test, then we've done it. The State Department's counting on our versatility. That's all we need, Justin—cleverness!"

Marner's eyes lit up. "Dave, I'm sorry I was so pigheaded a minute ago. We'll give them the business, all right!"

He stood up a little higher and gingerly extended a hand into the gaping servomechanism in the wall.

"What are you doing?" Kemridge asked.

"Never mind. Get on the phone and tell Plorvash that we'll be ready to get to work tomorrow. While you're doing that, I want to fool with this relay. Might as well get some practice now!" He was radiant with new-found enthusiasm.

When Plorvash knocked on the door the following morning, the mood was still on them. They were clear-eyed, wide awake, and firmly convinced they could master any problem.

"Who's there?" Marner asked loudly.

"Me," the Domerangi said. "Plorvash."

Instantly the door flew open and the dumfounded alien chargé d'affaires was confronted with the sight of the two Earthmen still snug in their beds. He peered behind the door and in the closet.

"Who opened the door?" he asked suspiciously.

Marner sat up in bed and grinned. "Try it again. Go outside and call out 'Plorvash' the way you just did."

The alien lumbered out, pulling the door shut behind him. When he was outside, he said his name again and the door opened immediately. He thundered across the threshold and looked from Marner to Kemridge. "What did you do?"

"We were experimenting with the door-opener last night," Kemridge said. "And before we put it back together, we decided it might be fun to rig up a modified vocoder circuit that would open the door automatically at the sound of the syllables 'Plorvash' directed at it from outside. It works very nicely."

The alien scowled. "Ah—yes. Very clever. Now as to

the terms of this test you two are to engage in: We've prepared a fully equipped laboratory for you in Central Sqorvik—that's a suburb not far from here—and we've set up two preliminary problems for you, as agreed. When you've dealt with those—*if* you've dealt with those—we'll give you a third."

"And if we don't deal with them successfully?"

"Why, then you'll have failed to demonstrate your ability."

"Reasonable enough," Marner said. "But just when do we *win* this thing? Do you go on giving us projects till we miss?"

"That would be the ultimate proof of your ability, wouldn't it?" Plorvash asked. "But you'll be relieved to know that we have no such plans. According to the terms of the agreement between ourselves and your government, the test groups on each planet will be required to carry out no more than three projects." The alien's two mouths smiled unpleasantly. "We'll consider successful completion of all three projects as ample proof of your ability."

"I don't like the way you say that," Kemridge objected. "What's up your sleeve?"

"My sleeve? I don't believe I grasp the idiom," Plorvash said.

"Never mind. Just a Terran expression," said Kemridge.

A car was waiting for them outside the hotel—a long, low job with a pulsating flexible hood that undulated in a distressing fashion, like a monstrous metal artery.

Plorvash slid the back door open. "Get in. I'll take you to the lab to get started."

Marner looked at the alien, then at Kemridge. Kemridge nodded. "How about one for the road?" Marner suggested.

"Eh?"

"Another idiom," he said. "I mean a drink. Alcoholic beverage. Stimulant of some kind. You catch?"

The alien grinned nastily. "I understand. There's a dispensary on the next street. We don't want to rush you on this thing, anyway." He pointed to the moving roadway. "Get aboard and we'll take a quick one."

They followed the Domerangi onto the moving strip and a moment later found themselves in front of a domed structure planted just off the roadway.

"It doesn't look very cozy," Kemridge commented as they entered. A pungent odor of ether hit their nostrils. Half a dozen Domerangi were lying on the floor, holding jointed metal tubes. As they watched, Plorvash clambered down and sprawled out on his back.

"Come join me," he urged. "Have a drink." He reached for a tube that slithered across the floor toward him and fitted it into his left feeding mouth.

"This is a bar?" Kemridge asked unhappily. "It looks more like the emergency ward of a hospital."

Plorvash finished drinking and stood up, wiping a few drops of green liquid from his jaw. "Good," he said. "It's not beer, but it's good stuff. I thought you two wanted to drink."

Marner sniffed the ether-laded air in dismay and shook his head. "We're not—thirsty. It takes time to get used to alien customs, I suppose."

"I suppose so," Plorvash agreed. "Very well, then. Let's go to the lab, shall we?"

The laboratory was, indeed, a sumptuous place. The two Earthmen stood at the entrance to the monstrous room and marveled visibly.

"We're impressed," Marner said finally to the Dome-rangi.

"We want to give you every opportunity to succeed," Plorvash said. "This is just as important for us as it is for you."

Marner took two or three steps into the lab and glanced around. To the left, an enormous oscilloscope wiggled greenly at him. The right-hand wall was bristling with elaborate servomechanisms of all descriptions. The far wall was a gigantic toolchest, and workbenches were spotted here and there. The lighting—indirect, of course—was bright and eye-easing. It was the sort of research setup a sane engineer rarely bothers even to dream of.

"You're making it too easy for us," said Kemridge. "It can't be hard to pull off miracles in a lab like this."

"We are honest people. If you can meet our tests, we'll grant that you're better than we are. *If* you can, that is. If you fail, it can't be blamed on poor working conditions."

"Fair enough," Kemridge agreed. "When are you ready to start?"

"Immediately." Plorvash reached into the bagging folds of his sash and withdrew a small plastic bubble, about four inches long, containing a creamy-white fluid.

"This is a depilator," he said. He squeezed a few drops out of the bubble into the spoonlike end of one tentacle and rubbed the liquid over the thick, heavy red beard that sprouted on his lower jaw. A streak of beard came away as he rubbed. "It is very useful." He handed the bubble to Marner. "Duplicate it."

"But we're engineers, not chemists," Marner protested.

"Never mind, Justin." Kemridge turned to the alien. "That's the first problem. Suppose you give us the second one at the same time, just to make things more convenient. That way, we'll each have one to work on."

Plorvash frowned. "You want to work on two projects at once? All right." He turned, strode out, and returned a few moments later, carrying something that looked like a large mousetrap inside a cage. He handed it to Kemridge.

"We use this to catch small house pests," Plorvash explained. "It's a self-baiting trap. Most of our house pests are color-sensitive and this trap flashes colors as a lure. For example, it does this to trap vorks—" he depressed a lever in the back and the trap glowed a lambent green— "and this to catch flaibs." Another lever went down and the trap radiated warm purple. An unmistakable odor of rotting vegetation emanated from it as well.

"It is, as you see, most versatile," the alien went on. "We've supplied you with an ample number of vermin of different sorts—they're at the back of the lab, in those cages—and you ought to be able to rig a trap to duplicate this one. At least, I hope you can."

"Is this all?" Kemridge asked.

Plorvash nodded. "You can have all the time you need. That was the agreement."

"Exactly," Kemridge said. "We'll let you know when we've gotten somewhere."

"Fine," said Plorvash.

After he had left, Marner squeezed a couple of drops of the depilatory out onto the palm of his hand. It stung and he immediately shook it off.

"Better not fool with that till we've run an analysis," Kemridge suggested. "If it's potent enough to remove Domerangi beards, it'll probably be a good skin-dissolver for Earthmen. Those babies have tough hides."

Marner rubbed his hand clean hastily. "What do you think of the deal in general?"

"Pretty soft," Kemridge said. "It shouldn't take more than a week to knock off both these things, barring complications. Seems to me they could pick tougher projects than these."

"Wait till the final one," warned Marner. "These are just warm-ups."

Four days later, Marner called Plorvash from the lab. The alien's bulky form filled the screen. "Hello," he said mildly. "What's new?"

"We've finished the job," Marner reported.

"Both of them?"

"Naturally."

"I'll be right over."

Plorvash strode into the lab about fifteen minutes later, and the two Earthmen, who were busy with the animal cages at the back of the lab, waved in greeting.

"Stay where you are," Kemridge called loudly. He reached up, pressed a switch, and thirty cages clanged open at once.

As a horde of Domerangi vermin came bounding, slithering, crawling, and rolling across the floor toward Plorvash, the alien leaped back in dismay. "What kind of trick is this?"

"Don't worry," Marner said, from the remotest corner of the lab. "It'll all be over in a second."

The animals ignored Plorvash and, to his surprise, they made a beeline for a complex, humming arrangement of gears and levers behind the door. As they approached, it began flashing a series of colors, emanating strange odors, and making curious clicking noises. When the horde drew closer, jointed arms suddenly sprang out and scooped them wholesale into a hopper that gaped open at floor level. Within a moment, they were all stowed away inside.

Marner came across the lab, followed by Kemridge. "We've improved on your model," he said. "We've built a better trap. Your version can deal with only one species at a time."

Plorvash gulped resoundingly. "Very nice. Quite remarkable, in fact."

"We have the schematics in our room," said Kemridge. "The trap may have some commercial value on Domerang."

"Probably," Plorvash admitted. "How'd you do on the depilator?"

"That was easy," Marner said. "With the setup you gave us, chemical analysis was a snap. Only I'm afraid we've improved on the original model there, too."

"What do you mean?"

Marner rubbed the side of his face uneasily. "I tried our stuff on myself, couple of days ago, and my face is still smooth as a baby's. The effect seems to be permanent."

"You'll submit samples, of course," Plorvash said. "But I think it's fairly safe to assume that you've passed through the first two projects—ah—reasonably well. Curiously, your counterparts on Earth also did well on their preliminaries, according to our Consul in New York."

"Glad to hear it," Marner lied. "But the third problem tells the tale, doesn't it?"

"Exactly," said Plorvash. "Let's have that one now, shall we?"

A few minutes later, Marner and Kemridge found themselves staring down at a complicated nest of glittering relays and tubes that seemed to power an arrangement of pistons and rods. Plorvash had carried it in with the utmost delicacy and had placed it on a workbench in the middle of the vast laboratory.

"What is it?" Marner asked.

"You'll see," promised the alien. He fumbled in the back of the machine, drew forth a cord, and plugged it into a wall socket. A small tube in the heart of the machine glowed cherry red and the pistons began to move, first slowly, then more rapidly. After a while, it was humming away at an even, steady clip, pistons barreling back and forth in purposeless but inexorable motion.

Kemridge bent and peered as close to the workings of the gadget as he dared. "It's an engine. What of it?"

"It's a special kind of engine," Plorvash said. "Suppose you take the plug out."

The Earthman worked the plug from its socket and looked at the machine. Then the plug dropped from his limp hand and skittered to the floor.

"It—doesn't stop going, does it?" Kemridge asked quietly. "The pistons keep on moving."

"This is our power source," Plorvash said smugly. "We use them in vehicles and other such things. It's the third problem."

"We'll give it a try," Marner tried to say casually.

"I'll be most interested in the results," Plorvash said. "And now I must bid you a good day."

"Sure," Marner said weakly. "Cheers."

They watched the broadbeamed alien waddle gravely out of the laboratory, waited till the door was closed, and glanced at the machine.

It was still moving.

Marner licked his lips and looked pleadingly at Kemridge. "Dave, can we build a perpetual-motion machine?"

The Domerangi machine worked just as well plugged in or unplugged, once it had tapped some power source to begin with. The pistons threaded ceaselessly up and down. The basic components of the thing seemed simple enough.

"The first step to take," Marner said, "is to shut the damned thing off so we can get a look at its innards."

"How do we do that?"

"By reversing the power source, I suppose. Feed a negative pulse through that power input and that ought to do it. We'll have to reverse the polarity of the signal."

Half an hour's hard work with the tools and solder had done that. They plugged the scrambled cord into the socket and the machine coughed twice and subsided.

"Okay," Marner said, rubbing his hands with an enthusiasm he did not feel. "Let's dig this baby apart and find out what makes it tick." He turned and stared meaningfully at Kemridge. "And let's adopt this as a working credo, Dave: inasmuch as the Domerangi have already built this thing, it's not impossible. Okay?"

"That seems to be the only basis we can approach it on," Kemridge agreed.

They huddled around the device, staring at the workings. Marner reached down and pointed at a part. "This thing is something like a tuned-plate feedback oscillator," he observed. "And I'll bet we've almost got a thyratron tube over here. Their technology's a good approximation of ours. In fact, the whole thing's within our grasp, technically."

"Hmm. And the result is a closed regenerative system with positive feedback," Kemridge said dizzily. "Infinite energy, going round and round the cycle. If you draw off a hundred watts or so—well, infinity minus a hundred is still infinity!"

"True enough." Marner wiped a gleaming bead of perspiration from his forehead. "Dave, we're going to have to puzzle this thing out from scratch. And we don't dare fail."

He reached doggedly for a screwdriver. "Remember our motto. We'll use our natural savvy and a little perspiration, and we ought to do it."

Three weeks later, they had come up with their first trial model—which wobbled along for half an hour, then gave up.

And a month after that, they had a machine that didn't give up.

Hesitantly, they sent for Plorvash.

"There it is," Marner said, pointing to the bizarre thing that stood next to the original model. Both machines were humming blithely, plugs dangling from the sockets.

"It works?" Plorvash whispered paling.

"It hasn't stopped yet," Marner said. There were heavy rings under his eyes and his usually plump face was drawn, with the skin tight over his cheekbones. It had been two months of almost constant strain and both Earthmen showed it.

"It works, eh?" Plorvash asked. "*How?*"

"A rather complex hyperspace function," Kemridge said. "I don't want to bother explaining it now—you'll find it all in our report—but it was quite a stunt in topology. We couldn't actually duplicate your model, but we achieved the same effect, which fulfills the terms of the agreement."

"All as a matter of response to challenge," said Marner. "We didn't think we could do it until we *had* to—so we did."

"I didn't think you could do it, either," Plorvash said hoarsely. He walked over and examined the machine closely. "It works, you say? Honestly, now?" His voice was strained.

"Of course," Marner said indignantly.

"We have just one question." Kemridge pointed to a small black rectangular box buried deep in a maze of circuitry in the original model. "That thing down there—it nearly threw us. We couldn't get it open and so we had to bypass it and substitute a new system for it. What in blazes is it?"

Plorvash wheeled solidly around to face them. "That," he said in a strangled voice, "is the power source. It's a miniature photoelectric amplifier that should keep the model running for—oh, another two weeks or so. Then the jig would have been up."

"How's that?" Marner was startled.

"It's time to explain something to you," the alien said wearily. *"We don't have any perpetual-motion machines.* You've been cruelly hoaxed into inventing one for us. It's dastardly, but we didn't really think you were going to do it. It took some of our best minds to rig up the model we gave you, you know."

Marner drew up a lab stool and sat down limply, white-faced. Kemridge remained standing, his features blank with disbelief.

Marner said, "You mean we invented the thing and you didn't—you—"

Plorvash nodded. "I'm just as astonished as you are," he said. He reached for a lab stool himself and sat down. It groaned under his weight.

Kemridge recovered first. "Well," he said after a moment of silence, "now that it's all over, we'll take our machine and go back to Earth. This invalidates the contest, of course."

"I'm afraid you can't do that," Plorvash said. "By a statute enacted some seven hundred years ago, any research done in a Domerangi government lab is automatically government property. Which means, of course, that we'll have to confiscate your—ahem—project."

"That's out of the question!" Marner said hotly.

"And, furthermore, we intend to confiscate *you*, too. We'd like you to stay and show us how to build our machines."

"This is cause for war," Kemridge said. "Earth won't let you get away with this—this kidnapping!"

"Possibly not. But in view of the way things have turned out, it's the sanest thing we can do. And I *don't* think Earth will go to war over you."

"We demand to see our Consul," said Marner.

"Very well," Plorvash agreed. "It's within your rights, I suppose."

The Earth Consul was a white-haired, sturdy gentleman named Culbertson, who arrived on the scene later that day.

"This is very embarrassing for all of us," the Consul said. He ran his hands nervously down his traditional pin-striped trousers, adjusting the crease.

"You can get us out of it, of course," Marner said. "That machine is our property and they have no right to keep us prisoners here to operate it, do they?"

"Not by all human laws. But the fact remains, unfortunately, that according to *their* laws, they have every right to your invention. And by the treaty of 2716, waiving extraterritorial sovereignty, Earthmen on Domerang are subject to Domerangi laws, and vice versa." He spread his hands in a gesture of sympathetic frustration.

"You mean we're stuck here," Marner said bluntly. He

shut his eyes, remembering the nightmare that was the Domerangi equivalent of a bar, thinking of the morbid prospect of spending the rest of his life on this unappetizing planet, all because of some insane dare. "Go on, tell us the whole truth."

The Consul put the palms of his hands together delicately. "We intend to make every effort to get you off, of course—naturally so, since we owe a very great debt to you two. You realize that you've upheld Earth's pride."

"Lot of good it did us," Marner grunted.

"Nevertheless, we feel anxious to make amends for the whole unhappy incident. I can assure you that we'll do everything in our power to make your stay here as pleasant and as restful as—"

"Listen, Culbertson," Kemridge said grimly. "We don't want a vacation here, not even with dancing girls twenty-four hours a day and soft violins in the background. We don't like it here. We want to go home. You people got us into this—now get us out."

The Consul grew even more unhappy-looking. "I wish you wouldn't put it that way. We'll do all we can." He paused for a moment, deep in thought, and said, "There's one factor in the case that we haven't as yet explored."

"What's that?" Marner asked uneasily.

"Remember the two Domerangi engineers who went to Earth on the other leg of this hookup?" The Consul glanced around the lab. "Is this place wired anywhere?"

"We checked," Kemridge said, "and you can speak freely. What do they have to do with us?"

Culbertson lowered his voice.

"There's a slim chance for you. I've been in touch with authorities on Earth and they've been keeping me informed of the progress of the two Domerangi. You know they got through their first two projects as easily as you did."

The two Earthmen nodded impatiently.

The old diplomat smiled his apologies. "I hate to admit this, but it seems the people at the Earth end of this deal had much the same idea the Domerangi did."

"Perpetual motion, you mean?"

"Not quite," Culbertson said. "They rigged up a phony anti-gravity machine and told the Domerangi to duplicate it just as was done here. Our psychologies must be similar."

"And what happened?" Marner asked.

"Nothing, yet," the Consul said sadly. "But they're still working on it, I'm told. If they're as clever as they say they are, they ought to hit it sooner or later. You'll just have to be patient and sweat it out. We'll see to it that you're well taken care of in the meantime, of course, and—"

"I don't get it. What does that have to do with us?" Marner demanded.

"If they keep at it, they'll invent it eventually."

Marner scowled. "That may take years. It may take forever. They may *never* discover a workable anti-grav. Then what about us?"

The Consul looked sympathetic and shrugged.

A curious gleam twinkled in Kemridge's eye. He turned to Marner. "Justin, do you know anything about tensor applications and gravitational fields?"

"What are you driving at?" Marner said.

"We've got an ideal lab setup here. And I'm sure those two Domerangi down there wouldn't mind taking credit for someone else's anti-grav, if they were approached properly. What do you think?"

Marner brightened. "That's right—they must be just as anxious to get home as we are!"

"You mean," said the Consul, "you'd build the machine and let us smuggle it to Earth so we could slip it to the Domerangi and use that as a talking-point for a trade and—"

He stopped, seeing that no one was listening to him, and looked around. Marner and Kemridge were at the far end of the lab, scribbling equations feverishly.

The Sixth Palace

...•—▸◉◂—•...

Ben Azai was deemed worthy and stood at the gate
of the sixth palace and saw the ethereal splendor of the
pure marble plates. He opened his mouth and said twice,
"Water! Water!" In the twinkling of an eye they decapi-
tated him and threw eleven thousand iron bars at him.
This shall be a sign for all generations that no one should
err at the gate of the sixth palace.

—*Lesser Hekhaloth*

THERE WAS THE treasure, and there was the guardian
of the treasure. And there were the whitened bones of
those who had tried in vain to make the treasure their own.
Even the bones had taken on a kind of beauty, lying out
there by the gate of the treasure vault, under the blazing
arch of the heavens. The treasure itself lent beauty to

everything near it—even the scattered bones, even the grim guardian.

The home of the treasure was a small world that belonged to red Valzar. Hardly more than moon-sized, really, with no atmosphere to speak of, a silent, dead little world that spun through darkness a billion miles from its cooling primary. A wayfarer had stopped there once. Where from, where bound? No one knew. He had established a cache there, and there it still lay, changeless and eternal, treasure beyond belief, presided over by the faceless metal man who waited with metal patience for his master's return.

There were those who would have the treasure. They came, and were challenged by the guardian, and died.

On another world of the Valzar system, men undiscouraged by the fate of their predecessors dreamed of the hoard, and schemed to possess it. Lipescu was one: a tower of a man, golden beard, fists like hammers, gullet of brass, back as broad as a tree of a thousand years. Bolzano was another: awlshaped, bright of eye, fast of finger, twig thick, razor sharp. They had no wish to die.

Lipescu's voice was like the rumble of island galaxies in collision. He wrapped himself around a tankard of good black ale and said, "I go tomorrow, Bolzano."

"Is the computer ready?"

"Programmed with everything the beast could ask me," the big man boomed. "There won't be a slip."

"And if there is?" Bolzano asked, peering idly into the blue, oddly pale, strangely meek eyes of the giant. "And if the robot kills you?"

"I've dealt with robots before."

Bolzano laughed. "That plain is littered with bones, friend. Yours will join the rest. Great bulky bones, Lipescu. I can see them now."

"You're a cheerful one, friend."

"I'm realistic."

Lipescu shook his head heavily. "If you were realistic, you wouldn't be in this with me," he said slowly. "Only a dreamer would do such a thing as this." One meaty paw hovered in the air, pounced, caught Bolzano's forearm. The little man winced as bones ground together. Lipescu said, "You won't back out? If I die, you'll make the attempt?"

"Of course I will, you idiot."

"Will you? You're a coward, like all little men. You'll watch me die, and then you'll turn tail and head for another part of the universe as fast as you know how. Won't you?"

"I intend to profit by your mistakes," Bolzano said in a clear, testy voice. "Let go of my arm."

Lipescu released his grip. The little man sank back in his chair, rubbing his arm. He gulped ale. He grinned at his partner and raised his glass.

"To success," Bolzano said.

"Yes. To the treasure."

"And to long life afterward."

"For both of us," the big man boomed.

"Perhaps," said Bolzano. "Perhaps."

He had his doubts. The big man was sly, Ferd Bolzano knew, and that was a good combination, not often found: slyness and size. Yet the risks were great. Bolzano wondered which he preferred—that Lipescu should gain the treasure on his attempt, thus assuring Bolzano of a share without risk, or that Lipescu should die, forcing Bolzano to venture his own life. Which was better, a third of the treasure without hazard, or the whole thing for the highest stake?

Bolzano was a good enough gambler to know the answer to that. Yet there was more than yellowness to the man; in his own way, he longed for the chance to risk his life on the airless treasure world.

Lipescu would go first. That was the agreement. Bolzano had stolen the computer, had turned it over to the big man, and Lipescu would make the initial attempt. If he gained the prize, his was the greater share. If he perished, it was Bolzano's moment next. An odd partnership, odd terms, but Lipescu would have it no other way, and Ferd Bolzano did not argue the point with his beefy compatriot. Lipescu would return with the treasure, or he would not return at all. There would be no middle way, they both were certain.

Bolzano spent an uneasy night. His apartment, in an airy shaft of a building overlooking glittering Lake Eris, was a comfortable place, and he had little longing to leave it. Lipescu, by preference, lived in the stinking slums beyond the southern shore of the lake, and when the two men parted for the night, they went in opposite ways. Bolzano considered bringing a woman home for the night, but did not. Instead, he sat moody and wakeful before the televector screen, watching the procession of worlds, peering at the green and gold and ochre planets as they sailed through the emptiness.

Toward dawn, he ran the tape of the treasure. Octave Merlin had made that tape, a hundred years before, as he orbited sixty miles above the surface of the airless little world. Now Merlin's bones bleached on the plain, but the tape had come home, and bootlegged copies commanded a high price in hidden markets. His camera's sharp eye had seen much.

There was the gate; there was the guardian. Gleaming, ageless, splendid. The robot stood ten feet high, a square, blocky, black shape topped by the tiny anthropomorphic head dome, featureless and sleek. Behind him the gate, wide open but impassable all the same. And behind him, the treasure, culled from the craftsmanship of a thousand worlds, left here who knew why, untold years ago.

No mere jewels. No dreary slabs of so-called precious metal. The wealth here was not intrinsic; no vandal would think of melting the treasure into dead ingots. Here were statuettes of spun iron, that seemed to move and breathe. Plaques of purest lead, engraved with lathework that dazzled the mind and made the heart hesitate. Cunning intaglios in granite, from the workshops of a frosty world half a parsec from nowhere. A scatter of opals, burning with an inner light, fashioned into artful loops of brightness.

A helix of rainbow-colored wood. A series of interlocking strips of some beast's bone, bent and splayed so that the pattern blurred and perhaps abutted some other-dimensional continuum. Cleverly carved shells, one within the other, descending to infinity. Burnished leaves of nameless trees. Polished pebbles from unknown beaches. A dizzying spew of wonders, covering some fifty square yards, sprawled out behind the gate in stunning profusion.

Rough men unschooled in the tenets of aesthetics had given their lives to possess the treasure. It took no fancy knowledge to realize the wealth of it, to know that collectors strung from galaxy to galaxy would fight with bare fangs to claim their share. Gold bars did not a treasure make. But these things? Beyond duplication, almost beyond price?

Bolzano was wet with a fever of yearning before the tape had run its course. When it was over, he slumped in his chair, drained, depleted.

Dawn came. The silvery moons fell from the sky. The

red sun splashed across the heavens. Bolzano allowed himself the luxury of an hour's sleep.

And then it was time to begin. . . .

As a precautionary measure, they left the ship in a
parking orbit three miles above the airless world. Past reports were unreliable, and there was no telling how far the
robot guardian's power extended. If Lipescu were successful, Bolzano could descend and get him—and the treasure.
If Lipescu failed, Bolzano would land and make his own
attempt.

The big man looked even bigger, encased in his suit
and in the outer casement of a dropshaft. Against his massive chest he wore the computer, an extra brain as lovingly
crafted as any object in the treasure hoard. The guardian
would ask him questions; the computer would help him
answer. And Bolzano would listen. If Lipescu erred, possibly his partner could benefit by knowledge of the error
and succeed.

"Can you hear me?" Lipescu asked.

"Perfectly. Go on, get going!"

"What's the hurry? Eager to see me die?"

"Are you lacking in confidence?" Bolzano asked. "Do
you want me to go first?"

"Fool," Lipescu muttered. "Listen carefully. If I die, I
don't want it to be in vain."

"What would it matter to you?"

The bulky figure wheeled around. Bolzano could not
see his partner's face, but he knew Lipescu must be scowl-
ing. The giant rumbled, "Is life that valuable? Can't I take
a risk?"

"For *my* benefit?"

"For mine," Lipescu said. "I'll be coming back."

"Go, then. The robot is waiting."

Lipescu walked to the lock. A moment later he was through and gliding downward, a one-man spaceship, jets flaring beneath his feet. Bolzano settled by the scanner to watch. A televector pickup homed in on Lipescu just as he made his landing, coming down in a blaze of fire. The treasure and its guardian lay about a mile away. Lipescu rid himself of the dropshaft, stepping with giant bounds toward the waiting guardian.

Bolzano watched.

Bolzano listened.

The televector pickup provided full fidelity. It was useful for Bolzano's purposes, and useful, too, for Lipescu's vanity, for the big man wanted his every moment taped for posterity. It was interesting to see Lipescu dwarfed by the guardian. The black faceless robt, squat and motionless, topped the big man by better than three feet.

Lipescu said, "Step aside."

The robot's reply came in surprisingly human tones, though void of any distinguishing accent. "What I guard is not to be plundered."

"I claim them by right," Lipescu said.

"So have many others. But their right did not exist. Nor does yours. I cannot step aside for you."

"Test me," Lipescu said. "See if I have the right or not!"

"Only my master may pass."

"Who is your master? *I* am your master!"

"My master is he who can command me. And no one can command me who shows ignorance before me."

"Test me, thcn," Lipescu demanded.

"Death is the penalty for failure."

"Test me."

"The treasure does not belong to you."

"Test me and step aside."

"Your bones will join the rest here."

"Test me," Lipescu said.

Watching from aloft, Bolzano went tense. His thin body drew together like that of a chilled spider. Anything might happen now. The robot might propound riddles, like the Sphinx confronting Oedipus.

It might demand proofs of mathematical theorems. It might ask the translation of strange words. So they gathered, from their knowledge of what had befallen other men here. And, so it seemed, to give the wrong answer was to earn instant death.

He and Lipescu had ransacked the libraries of the world. They had packed all knowledge, so they hoped, into their computer. It had taken months, even with multistage programming. The tiny globe of metal on Lipescu's chest contained an infinity of answers to an infinity of questions.

Below, there was a long silence as man and robot studied one another. Then the guardian said, "Define latitude."

"Do you mean geographical latitude?" Lipescu asked.

Bolzano congealed with fear. The idiot, asking for a clarification! He would die before he began!

The robot said, "Define latitude."

Lipescu's voice was calm. "The angular distance of a point on a planet's surface north or south of the equator, as measured from the center of the planet."

"Which is more consonant," the robot asked, "the minor third or the major sixth?"

There was a pause. Lipescu was no musician. But the computer would feed him the answer.

"The minor third," Lipescu said.

Without a pasue, the robot fired another question.

"Name the prime numbers between five thousand two hundred and thirty-seven and seven thousand six hundred and forty-one."

Bolzano smiled as Lipescu handled the question with ease. So far, so good. The robot had stuck to strictly factual questions, schoolbook stuff, posing no real problems to Lipescu. And after the initial hesitation and quibble over latitude, Lipescu had seemed to grow in confidence from moment to moment. Bolzano squinted at the scanner, looking beyond the robot, through the open gate, to the helter-skelter pile of treasures. He wondered which would fall to his lot when he and Lipescu divided them, two-thirds for Lipescu, the rest for him.

"Name the seven tragic poets of Elifora," the robot said.

Domiphar, Halionis, Slegg, Hork-Sekan. . . ."

"The fourteen signs of the zodiac as seen from Morneez," the robot demanded.

"The Teeth, the Serpents, the Leaves, the Waterfall, the Blot. . . ."

"What is a pedicel?"

"The stalk of an individual flower of an inflorescence."

"How many years did the Siege of Larrina last?"

"Eight."

"What did the flower cry in the third canto of Somner's *Vehicles*?"

" 'I ache, I sob, I whimper, I die,' " Lipescu boomed.

"Distinguish between the stamen and the pistil."

"The stamen is the pollen-producing organ of the flower; the pistil. . . ."

And so it went. Question after question. The robot was not content with the legendary three questions of mythology; it asked a dozen, and then asked more. Lipescu answered perfectly, prompted by the murmuring of the peerless compendium of knowledge strapped to his chest. Bolzano kept careful count: The big man had dealt magnificently with seventeen questions. When would the robot concede defeat? When would it end its grim quiz and step aside?

It asked an eighteenth question, pathetically easy. All it wanted was an exposition of the Pythagorean theorem. Lipescu did not even need the computer for that. He answered, briefly, concisely, correctly. Bolzano was proud of his burly partner.

Then the robot struck Lipescu dead.

It happened in the flickering of an eyelid. Lipescu's voice had ceased, and he stood there, ready for the next question, but the next question did not come. Rather, a panel in the robot's vaulted belly slid open, and something bright and sinuous lashed out, uncoiling over the ten feet or so that separated guardian from challenger, and sliced Lipescu in half. The bright something slid back out of sight. Lipescu's trunk toppled to one side. His massive legs remained absurdly planted for a moment; then they crumpled, and a spacesuit leg kicked once, and all was still.

Stunned, Bolzano trembled in the loneliness of the cabin, and his lymph turned to water. What had gone wrong? Lipescu had given the proper answer to every question, and yet the robot had slain him. Why? Could the big man possibly have misphrased Pythagoras? No: Bolzano had listened. The answer had been flawless, as had the seventeen that preceded it. Seemingly the robot had lost patience with the game, then. The robot had cheated. Arbitrarily, maliciously, it had lashed out at Lipescu, punishing him for the correct answer.

Did robots cheat, Bolzano wondered? Could they act in malicious spite? No robot he knew was capable of such actions; but this robot was unlike all others.

For a long while, Bolzano remained huddled in the cabin. The temptation was strong to blast free of orbit and head home, treasureless but alive. Yet the treasure called to him. Some suicidal impulse drove him on. Sirenlike, the robot drew him downward.

There had to be a way to make the robot yield, Bolzano thought, as he guided his small ship down to the broad barren plain. Using the computer had been a good idea, whose only defect was that it hadn't worked. The records were uncertain, but it appeared that in the past, men had died when they finally gave a wrong answer after a series of right ones. Lipescu had given no wrong answers. Yet he too had died. It was inconceivable that the robot understood some relationship of the squares on the hypotenuse and on the other two sides that was different from the relationship Lipescu had expressed.

Bolzano wondered what method would work.

He plodded leadenly across the plain toward the gate and its guardian. The germ of an idea formed in him, as he walked doggedly on.

He was, he knew, condemned to death by his own greed. Only extreme agility of mind would save him from sharing Lipescu's fate. Ordinary intelligence would not work. Odyssean cleverness was the only salvation.

Bolzano approached the robot. Bones lay everywhere. Lipescu weltered in his own blood. Against that vast dead chest lay the computer, Bolzano knew. But he shrank from reaching for it. He would do without it. He looked away, unwilling to let the sight of Lipescu's severed body interfere with the coolness of his thoughts.

He collected his courage. The robot showed no interest in him.

"Give ground," Bolzano said. "I am here. I come for the treasure."

"Win your right to it."

"What must I do?"

"Demonstrate truth," the robot said. "Reveal inwardness. Display understanding."

"I am ready," said Bolzano.

The robot offered a question. "What is the excretory unit of the vertebrate kidney called?"

Bolzano contemplated. He had no idea. The computer could tell him, but the computer lay strapped to the fallen Lipescu. No matter. The robot wanted truth, inwardness, understanding. These things were not necessarily the same as information. Lipescu had offered information. Lipescu had perished.

"The frog in the pond," Bolzano said, "utters an azure cry."

There was silence. Bolzano watched the robot's front, waiting for the panel to slide open, the sinuous something to chop him in half.

The robot said, "During the War of Dogs on Vanderverr IX, the embattled colonists drew up thirty-eight dogmas of defiance. Quote the third, the ninth, the twenty-second, and the thirty-fifth."

Bolzano pondered. This was an alien robot, product of an unknown hand. How did its maker's mind work? Did it respect knowledge? Did it treasure facts for their own sake? Or did it recognize that information is meaningless, insight a nonlogical process?

Lipescu had been logical. He lay in pieces.

"The mereness of pain," Bolzano responded, "is ineffable and refreshing."

The robot said, "The monastery of Kwaisen was besieged by the soldiers of Oda Nobunaga on the third of April, 1582. What words of wisdom did the abbot utter?"

Bolzano spoke quickly and buoyantly. "Eleven, forty-one, elephant, voluminous."

The last word slipped from his lips despite an effort to retrieve it. Elephants *were* voluminous, he thought. A fatal slip? The robot did not appear to notice.

Sonorously, ponderously, the great machine delivered the next question.

"What is the percentage of oxygen in the atmosphere of Muldonar VII?"

"False witness bears a swift sword," Bolzano replied.

The robot made an odd humming sound. Abruptly it rolled on massive treads, moving some six feet to its left. The gate of the treasure trove stood wide, beckoning.

"You may enter," the robot said.

Bolzano's heart leaped. He had won! He had gained the high prize!

Others had failed, most recently less than an hour before, and their bones glistened on the plain. They had tried to answer the robot, sometimes giving right answers, sometimes giving wrong ones, and they had died. Bolzano lived.

It was a miracle, he thought. Luck? Shrewdness? Some of each, he told himself. He had watched a man give eighteen right answers and die. So the accuracy of the responses did not matter to the robot. What did? Inwardness. Understanding. Truth.

There could be inwardness and understanding and truth in random answers, Bolzano realized. Where earnest striving had failed, mockery had succeeded. He had staked his life on nonsense, and the prize was his.

He staggered forward into the treasure trove. Even in

the light gravity, his feet were like leaden weights. Tension ebbed in him. He knelt among the treasures.

The tapes, the sharp-eyed televector scanners, had not begun to indicate the splendor of what lay here. Bolzano stared in awe and rapture at a tiny disk, no greater in diameter than a man's eye, on which myriad coiling lines writhed and twisted in patterns of rare beauty. He caught his breath, sobbing with the pain of perception, as a gleaming marble spire, angled in mysterious swerves, came into view. Here, a bright beetle of some fragile waxy substance rested on a pedestal of yellow jade. There, a tangle of metallic cloth spurted dizzying patterns of luminescence. And over there—and beyond—and there—

The ransom of a universe, Bolzano thought.

It would take many trips to carry all this to his ship. Perhaps it would be better to bring the ship to the hoard, eh? He wondered, though, if he would lose his advantage if he stepped back through the gate. Was it possible that he would have to win entrance all over again? And would the robot accept his answers as willingly the second time? It was something he would have to chance, Bolzano decided. His nimble mind worked out a plan. He would select a dozen of the finest treasures, as much as he could comfortably carry, and take them back to the ship. Then he would lift the ship and set it down next to the gate. If the robot raised objections about his entering, Bolzano would simply depart, taking what he had already secured. There was no point in running undue risks. When he had sold this cargo, and felt pinched for money, he could always return and try to win admission once again. Certainly, no one else would steal the horde if he abandoned it.

Selection, that was the key now.

Crouching, Bolzano picked through the treasure, choosing for portability and easy marketability. The marble spire? Too big. But the coiling disk, yes, certainly, and the beetle, of course, and this small statuette of dull hue, and the cameos showing scenes no human eye had ever beheld, and this, and this, and this—

His pulse raced. His heart thundered. He saw himself traveling from world to world, vending his wares. Collectors, museums, governments would vie with one another to have these prizes. He would let them bid each object up into the millions before he sold. And, of course, he would keep one or two for himself—or perhaps three or four—souvenirs of this great adventure.

And someday when wealth bored him he would return and face the challenge again. And he would dare the robot to question him, and he would reply with random absurdities, demonstrating his grasp on the fundamental insight that in knowledge there is only hollow merit, and the robot would admit him once more to the treasure trove.

Bolzano rose. He cradled his lovelies in his arms. Carefully, carefully, he thought. Turning, he made his way through the gate.

The robot had not moved. It had shown no interest as Bolzano plundered the hoard. The small man walked calmly past it.

The robot said, "Why have you taken those? What do you want with them?"

Bolzano smiled. Nonchalantly he replied, "I've taken them because they're beautiful. Because I want them. Is there a better reason?"

"No," the robot said, and the panel slid open in its ponderous black chest.

Too late, Bolzano realized that the test had not yet

ended, that the robot's question had arisen out of no idle curiosity. And this time he had replied in earnest, speaking in rational terms.

Bolzano shrieked. He saw the brightness coming toward him.

Death followed instantly.

Translation Error

※──◉──※

SEVERAL STRANGE OBJECTS were glittering in the amber depths of his detector plate, and Karn felt a gnawing uneasiness. It was only a few minutes after the ship's conversion out of the null-continuum onto the world-line of Earth, after the long nullspace voyage from Karn's distant home world.

Absent-mindedly Karn let his body cells flow into the Earther shape he had worn on his last visit, almost fifty years earlier, while he brooded over the rapidly moving objects in the detector plate. They seemed to be small bodies locked in orbit round the blue-green world below. They made no sense at all. The obvious explanation was that they were artificial planetary satellites, but surely that was impossible! Nine tiny metal moons, each in its own elliptical orbit—the implications of that made Karn feel sick. Earth could *not* have reached this stage along the technological scale yet, he told himself flatly. His computations could not have erred.

Or could they have?

Karn felt a chill invading his limbs. He went about the routine business of setting up his one-man ship for a landing and tried to forget the annoying existence of those nine artificial satellites. Rapidly he converted to planetary drive, switching off the nullspace translator that had brought him along the megaparsec-wide gulf between his home world and Earth, and headed into the descending series of spiraling orbits that would land him.

Artificial statellites, he thought dismally. *How could such a thing be?*

Karn checked the flow of despair that threatened to overwhelm him. What had been done could be undone again; if Earth somehow had reached the threshold of space despite all his careful work in 1916, he would simply have to take steps to correct that trend. He wondered who it was that had put the satellites up. The Germans, obviously. Scientifically and politically, they would be dominating the Earth in the year—what was it?—1959.

Yes, it had to be the Germans. America had the technologically inclined minds, but America, slumbering behind its 180 years of isolation, would hardly have any interest in conquering space. The Americans hardly knew there were other nations on their own world, let alone whole other worlds.

And no other nation seemed likely candidates for ownership of the accursed satellites. Certainly not France or Britain, crushed under the kaiser's heel in 1916. Nor old medieval Russia, comfortably vegetating beneath the czar. Italy? Austria–Hungary?

Possibly Japan, he thought. The Japanese might have put the things up.

But, Karn realized drearily, neither Germany nor Japan had as much as developed efficient airpower in 1916; it was incredible that in a bare forty-odd years they could have hurled orbiting satellites into space. Such a technological advance could have been stimulated only by war.

And, thought Karn, unless his computations were wrong for the first time in centuries, there had been no war on Earth since 1916, since the Treaty of Düsseldorf. He had carefully arranged things the last time. By keeping America out of the war, he had ensured German triumph, German dominion over all western Europe. His computations had predicted at least seventy years of peace before the broken revolutionary movement in Russia at last recovered its strength, hurled the czar from his throne, and challenged Germany's dominance. On his last visit he had removed the stimulus of immediate war. Yet space satellites circled the Earth.

Something had gone wrong, Karn thought bleakly. But given time he could put things to rights again.

His ship sliced down into the upper layers of the atmosphere. To his surprise, he discovered that the radioactivity of Earth's atmosphere had increased remarkably in the last forty years. Did that mean that the Earthers had unleashed nuclear energy *too*?

Something was very wrong. Karn feared he had plenty of work on his hands.

His original plans had called for him to make a landing in America, and for the moment he did not intend to alter those plans. He made the landing under cover of scramblers; forty years ago such pains had been unnecessary, but who knew now what sort of technology these Earthers had developed? For all he knew they had developed a detector system, too. It would be ignominious for him to be blasted out of the sky as a possible attacker. And until he had found out what the state of things was on Earth, it was madness to take risks. He landed under scramblers, totally impervious to detection. A neutrino-detector might have spotted him successfully—but, thought Karn, if they had invented neutrino-detectors, too, he might just as well turn around and go back to Hethivar with the doleful news that Terran invaders would be on their way sooner than they had dreamed. The neutrino screen came *much* later in a planet's development. Normal races didn't go from animal-drawn buggies to neutrino screens in fifty years, Karn thought.

Normal races didn't go from buggies to atomics and orbital satellites in fifty years either, Karn reflected. But who said these Earthers were normal?

He landed the ship in a pleasantly green meadow in the state across the river from New York. He could remember New York, all right, but the other state's name eluded him for the moment. New Guernsey? New Calais? Ah! *New Jersey.* That was it. He left the ship parked in New Jersey, having first keyed in the external scrambler that rotated the ship one-quarter turn out of the world-line. It wavered and vanished. No one would find it where it was now, though Karn could restore it to the continuum with a minimal outlay of energy, whenever he pleased.

His first step was to transport himself autokinetically across the river into New York City. The city had grown somewhat since 1916, but he had expected that. His extrapolation had foretold a building boom trending toward giantism. It was relieving to find one aspect of Earth following expectation.

The Hethivarian hovered invisibly over a Manhattan street long enough to pick out a likely entity for duplication. He would need a working identity while he was here.

He chose a man almost at random from a group of identically clad humans in gray suits and entered his mind long enough to duplicate the information he needed. Withdrawing, Karn made the necessary transformation and allowed himself to materialize.

Now he wore contemporary American clothes and the contemporary close-cropped hair style. In the trouser pocket of his flannel suit was a wallet duplicating in every respect that of the unsuspecting individual walking ahead. Karn had an ample supply of currency now—the paper money was smaller in size than it had been, Karn noted— as well as the necessary documents for survival and a ready-made familiarity with current events and contemporary slang.

He had no desire to encroach on the identity of the man he had momentarily entered, and so as he walked along he made minor alterations in the body he wore, thickening the ears, adding a mustache, deepening the facial lines. He increased the body weight by about a fifth. No one would mistake him for the other now.

All right, he thought. He could bluff the rest of the way. *Now to catch up on news events since 1916, and see just how I could have been so wrong.*

Karn already had a picture of the way Earth *should* have looked. He had spent several years on the planet in the past, rushing there in 1914 at the outbreak of war and rapidly healing the breaches until peace became possible two years later.

From his own extrapolations and from the computed results, he had expected the German Empire to be the world's dominant state, fat with its network of global colonies, replete with conquest and sanely satiated. Germany had all the territory it wanted or needed; it would embark on no campaign of world conquest. The status would remain quo. America, having been kept out of the Great War by Karn's careful intervention, would have clasped the Monroe Doctrine to itself even more firmly and would have shut itself away from the troublesome world out across the oceans. Russia would be drowsing under the yoke of the czar. Peace would pervade the Earth.

A pleasant peace, an era of good feelings.

Karn's motive was simple. The first scouts visiting Earth, more than a century before, had reported a vigorous and appallingly inventive race, just entering its mechanical age. The computed extrapolations had given the Hethivarian Network its biggest jolt in a millennium. They showed that Earth would be twice convulsed by war in the next century, each time taking a giant stride up the technological ladder. Without external meddling, the Earthers would leap right into the space age with frightening speed. Probabilities showed a 32 percent chance that the quarrelsome Earthers would destroy themselves in a hundred years—and a 68 percent chance that they would not, but instead would channel their dynamic forces and leap outward.

Extrapolations indicated that in a mere five centuries the Earthers would be, unless they managed to destroy themselves meanwhile, colonizing the stars—challenging the might of the age-old Hethivarian Network itself!

It was a frightening thought, indeed. In five centuries the Earthers would accomplish what it had taken Hethivar untold millenniums to do. They had to be stopped, for the sake of the galactic balance.

A little study showed that there were two ways to stop the Earthmen—and since one, the immediate obliteration of Earth by ultrabomb, was utterly repugnant to the highly civilized Hethivarians, there actually was only one way open. Internal intervention was called for. A trained Hethivarian agent would have to go to Earth and ease the pressures, turn down the steam under the kettle, pull back on the reins.

All that needed to be done was to remove the stimulus of war, which led to technological upspurts. A placid and untroubled Earth might sink into an amiably slothful way of life; the fierce spark that burned there might die down. So Karn was sent, and Karn engineered a peace. Not a lasting peace, of course—Earth would not be ready for that for a long time—but a stopgap, good for sixty or seventy years. When the next crisis arrived, it could be dealt with the same way. And the next, and the next, and the next—and so on into the distant future, if necessary. It was a sound plan. It would keep the Earthers from barking at the gates of the Network for centuries. It would maintain the calm balance of peace that had existed in the universe for so many thousands of years.

But, thought Karn, something had slipped up.

He would have to find a library and check up on recent history. First, though, he decided to purchase a newspaper. Entering his borrowed memory, he learned that newspapers could be bought with small silver coins. They were sold along the streets.

Karn pulled change from his pocket, selected a dime, and bought a *Times*. He scanned the front page rapidly.

Cold terror rippled through him.

Monstrous! he thought in baffled shock.

The headlines screamed incomprehensible things at him:

PRESIDENT CALLS FOR INCREASE IN FOREIGN AID
RUSSIA TURNS DOWN NEW PARLEY OFFER
SATELLITE LAUNCHING POSTPONED ONE WEEK
H-BOMB TEST A SUCCESS, WHITE HOUSE SAYS
GERMANS COOL TO REUNIFICATION HINTS

After the first instant of disorientation was over, Karn made the necessary adjustments in his metabolism to calm himself. The newspaper was a journal of a world of nightmares. He found himself near a small park breaking up the busy streets, and on uncertain legs he made his way to a bench and sat heavily down.

Next to him a stubblefaced man said, "You look sick, buddy. Everything okay?"

Karn had enough control of himself to find the right words. "My horse didn't make it, that's all. Stay away from sure things."

"A-men, pal!"

Karn smiled to himself. It was good to know he could handle a Terran colloquial conversation so skillfully. But the smile vanished as he returned his attention to the newspaper. He read it carefully and in detail, memorizing blocks of information as he went, and within fifteen minutes he had read his way through from end to end and could begin shaping the scattered data into a pattern.

Everything had gone completely haywire.

Germany was a fifth-rate country now, not the kingpin. Apparently there had been some sort of second Great War in the past few decades; Germany had been beaten and now lay helplessly divided. The powers on Earth today were the United States and Russia, glaring at each other menacingly in an uneasy stalemate.

Technological development had been catastrophically rapid. The infernal creatures had not only developed fission weapons but fusion ones as well, and evidently fission-fusion-fission bombs to boot. Work was progressing on control of thermonuclear energy.

And, spurred on by the threat of atomic war, a vast missile program was under way, and almost as a byproduct of the arms race, space was being conquered. The unbelievable Earthers had hoisted more than a dozen space satellites into orbit, and work was advancing on the problem of reaching the Moon by rocket.

Karn's mind automatically supplied the gloomy extrapolation. The Moon in ten years or less, the other planets by the end of the century, then a lull while a nullspace drive is invented, and then the conquest of the stars. Exactly as the first scouts had foreseen a century ago, only faster. How could this be possible? All his work of 1914–16 had gone completely to waste. If anything, things were worse than they would have been if he hadn't meddled.

None of it made any sense.

Karn knew what he had to do now. First, find a library and discover how this state of affairs had come about. Second, contact Hethivar by subradio and report on the situation. If ever there were a case for passing the buck, this was it. Something had to be done, and fast. But Karn was in no mood for making top-level decisions. Right now it was all he could do to cling to his sanity in the face of what had happened.

He found the nearest library and located a bulky world history, and scanned it rapidly, beginning in the mid-nineteenth century and working forward. When he was finished, he was as close to sheer panic as he had ever been in his long life. It was an effort simply to hang on to his physical manifestation and keep from wavering. It was necessary for him to go through all nine of the Stabilizing Exercises, one after another—a humiliating experience for one who had always prided himself on his coolness.

But yet what he had discovered could easily have destabilized a lesser man.

Terran history ran precisely as it should have run, right up to 1914. In the latter half of the nineteenth century, the pressures of industrialization and the stresses of up-surging nationalism had built up conflicts certain to erupt into war. That was as expected. In 1914, the war had broken out. That, too, was acceptable. The Hethivarian Planners had decided to permit the war to begin, as a sort of catharsis for the Earthmen, but to end the war before any serious changes in the Terran way of life could be brought about.

Yet the war had *not* ended at Düsseldorf in 1916, Karn discovered. Maddeningly, there was no mention of the Allied surrender nor of the Treaty of Düsseldorf. Instead, the Germans had gone ahead and provoked America into entering the war in 1917; almost simultaneously, the Russian revolutionists had successfully overthrown the czar. It was an unbelievable jolt to read of Germany's defeat, then of the foolish and suicidal peace settlement of 1919.

Defeated Germany had rebuilt its strength, with a mad-man named Hitler feeding on wounded national pride. And Russia had blindingly leaped into the twentieth century, shedding its medieval past and becoming an important world power overnight. Then, a second war, America drawn once again—and this time permanently—from its isolationist shell, Germany and its new ally Japan decisively crushed, Russia advancing to dominate half the world, atomic weapons actually used in battle—

Nightmare, Karn thought.

He searched through rows of books, hoping to find but one mention of the Treaty of Düsseldorf, his masterpiece, which had brought all Terran friction to a halt. Not one index had an entry of that sort. Panic assailed him. His grip on the universe tottered.

It was as if he had never come to Earth to end the Great War. Not one of his interventions had as much as survived in the pages of history. And matters stood at a dreadful impasse right now. The Earthers had already conquered space—twenty years ahead of the original extrapolation, a century or more ahead of Karn's revised estimate.

Earth hovered on the brink of self-destruction. That would be too bad for Earth, Karn thought. But—far worse for the galaxy as a whole—Earth also hovered at the edge of its space age. Nightmare of nightmares!

Hethivar had to be told of this. Immediately, before Karn could make another move. Hethivar had to know.

It was a simple matter to enter a washroom on the third floor of the library building and depart autokinetically for the New Jersey meadow. No one had seen him enter the washroom, and so no one would be perturbed by his failure to come out.

Arriving at the meadow with virtual instantaneity, Karn activated the scrambler key long enough for him to enter his ship, then once again returned to concealment. Switching on the subspace communicator, he framed a message to the Hethivarian Planners:

Esteemed Sirs—

The report of Karn 1832j4, assigned to Terran Manipulation. Good sirs, matters here have reached an unaccountable state. Manipulation activity of the previous visit has been totally negated. The Earthers have fought a second war and now have developed atomic weapons and orbital satellites.

Our worst fears have come to pass. Unless immediate action is taken the Earthers will be knocking at our gates within a century.

I am unable to explain the failure of the previous mission. Obviously we must restudy our entire science of probability. But one conclusion is certain; no amount of manipulation can halt the trends already set in motion. Our only course now is a drastic one. If we are to prevent the Earthers from entering space, we may no longer strive to check war on Earth, but rather now we must foment it.

It would be a simple matter of elementary tactics for me to instigate an atomic war on Earth, considering the uneasy international condition here. Such a war would probably not result in total destruction of Terran life, but would certainly set them back many hundreds of years. Of course, this drastic step contravenes our general ethical pattern, and so I dare not take action of this sort without your permission. Yet, good sirs, surely you will see that the destiny of the galaxy is at stake here. I will await your word.

He added his wavelength, so they would be able to reach him with a reply, and signed off.

There, he thought. *That should make them sweat a little!*

Subspace communication was not quite instantaneous. There would be a lag of several minutes before the Planners received his message, and it might be hours before they had decided on their reply. Well, a few hours were not likely to make much difference. He sat back to wait.

Touching off the atomic war would be child's play, he thought. All it took was a spark in the tinder—an atomic explosion obliterating some large American or Russian city, preferably both. Within minutes, jittery defense bases would send the missiles flying. Karn's nature was such that he found the idea of such a war repugnant. But yet, if it were necessary—

He still could not understand how his calculations had gone so far astray. Bitterly he saw that it had been a mistake to allow Earth fifty years of nonintervention; there should have been a Hethivarian agent here every moment of the time. Instead Hethivar had complacently relied on its extrapolations. As he looked back, it seemed an enormously shortsighted way of handling the situation. But they had been so *confident*. Well, second sight never helped anyone, Karn thought. The only path left was the barbarous but mandatory one of smashing Earth, or rather causing Earth to smash itself.

But—

His reflections were cut off by the whirring sound of the subradio printer. A message coming back so soon? Why, they had barely had time to consider! Obviously they had met at once and voted him carte blanche.

The message said:

> Karn, you blasted idiot—
> Are you out of your head? Your message makes no sense at all. Your job is to avoid that atomic war, not to touch it off. And what's this jabber about preventing the Earthers from entering space? Why

should we do that? And why did you change your wavelength?

Since you seem to have taken leave of your senses, you are to return to Hethivar at once. A replacement will be sent out. And if you meddle destructively in Terran affairs you'll get immediate personality disruption when we catch you.

If this is your idea of a joke, be advised that we aren't amused. You'd better have a good explanation when you get back here.

Adric
For the Planners

Bewildered, Karn let the message slip through numb fingers. He fought to restabilize himself, and had to run through the nine Stabilizing Exercises twice. This jolt, coming on top of the earlier one, left him reeling. Had the whole universe gone mad? He was dumbfounded by Adric's message. What was he talking about? What did he mean?

Karn pondered a return message. He had gotten no further than *Highly Esteemed Sirs* when his mind unmistakably detected Hethivarian life-impressions somewhere on the planet.

His outlines blurred in dazed puzzlement. No other Hethivarian was supposed to be within a parsec of Earth at this time. True, Adric had said something about a replacement being shipped out—but it took many weeks to make the trip from Hethivar to Earth. Who could the stranger be? Cautiously, Karn extended a tendril of perception—

—encountered another mind, a Hethivarian mind—

—touched—

—recoiled in shock.

The stranger was himself!

There had been no doubt about it. Their minds had met for only a microsecond, but yet Karn had learned that the other was one Karn 1832j4, newly arrived on Earth to engage in manipulation. He had touched the surface of that other mind, and its thought-forms were his thought-forms.

Karn gripped the walls of his ship and waited for the universe to stop spinning around him. This was what insanity was like, he thought.

A quiet voice said, "Would you mind telling me just who the devil you are?"

Karn realized the other being had come to him. He smiled and said, "You're a hallucination. Go away."

"I'm Karn. And so are you, it seems."

The other wore the body of an Earther, somewhat older, paunchy, balding. But as Karn watched, the Earther's visage gave way, in an instantaneous transition, to Karn's own. It was not like looking in the mirror, for the mirror reverses an image. This was the actual face of Karn, unfamiliar to him since he had never looked upon it in this fashion.

"We can't both be Karn," Karn said hoarsely.

"Have a look," the stranger replied, and extended his mind once again. Karn was reluctant to blend a second time; he attempted a barrier, but he was too late, and their minds joined. Karn looked deep. He saw his own thoughts laid out as neatly as he kept them, all his own memories of Hethivar. Yes, the other was himself.

But yet not himself. For mingled with the familiar memories were a host of unfamiliar ones. The other had arrived on Earth only minutes before, it seemed. But this was his third or fourth visit. He came to Earth regularly; his job was to protect the planet, to keep it from doing real harm to itself, to guide Earth along into space and into brotherhood with Hethivar.

It was like looking into a distorting mirror.

"You're here to aid Earth," Karn said.

"Yes. And you to destroy it. Destroy or else cripple. To keep the Earthers bottled up on their own world, where they can't harm the Network."

"And you're me," Karn said. "And I'm you. But we're opposite."

"Curious, isn't it? And what's this Treaty of Düsseldorf that stands out so in your mind?"

Karn said, "I arranged it, in 1916. It was supposed to provide Earth with long-lasting peace."

"To turn the Earthers into a bunch of sleepy vegetables, you mean. To rob them of the inner conflicts that would drive them into space eventually."

"And you *want* Earth to spread into space?"

"Of course," the other Karn said. "That's been our policy ever since our scouts saw the Earthers' potential. They're potentially the finest thing the universe has ever produced—but they have flaws. So we help them overcome their flaws. You think the Hethivarian Network is going to last forever?"

"No, but—"

"So why fight the inevitable? We recognize that the Earthers are potentially the next rulers of the galaxy. Okay. We take it gracefully and bow out. We don't attempt the hopeless job of trying to hold them down forever, nor do we destroy them now while we think we can. I'm here to simmer down some of their energy—to keep them from blowing themselves up, but to make sure that they rechannel those boiling drives of theirs *outward*, toward space. They're heading that way now. The Planners sent me here to make sure they get there."

Karn had never heard such a recital of insanity before in his life. But he saw clearly what had happened now. He knew why none of the history books mentioned the Treaty of Düsseldorf.

"I'm in trouble," he said.

"I'll bet you are!"

"Somehow I shifted out of my own world-line when leaving nullspace. I don't belong here at all."

Brusquely Karn made his way past the other to the control chamber. Sitting down at the control panel, he ran off a quick recheck of all the facts that had governed his conversion from the null-continuum onto Earth's world-line. It took only a few moments to find the discrepancy. He looked up at the other, his heart leaden.

"Find your mistake?" the other asked.

Karn's facial tendrils quivered in self-annoyance and shame. "Yes. I made a translation error of nearly one percent. I came out along the wrong world-line. This isn't my universe."

"Of course not."

"And that explains why everything seemed so wrong here. The Earth *I* knew would never have sent up space satellites, nor discovered atomics. The Earth I knew would be a peaceful world."

"A vegetating world," the other snapped scornfully.

Karn scowled at him. "A world that poses no threat to the Hethivarian Network, at any rate. I'm glad this isn't *my* world-line. I'd hate to be alive when the Earthmen come swarming over our world and make us slaves. And you'll have no one to thank but yourselves."

"We'll take the risk," the other Karn rejoined sourly. "But what do *you* plan to do now?"

"Get out of this insane world-line and back to my own, as fast as I can. I have important work to do."

"Suppressing Earth's culture?"

"Insuring Hethivar's future," Karn said thinly. He went on, "I sent a message back to the Planners a little while ago. They thought it came from you, and since it didn't make any sense they ordered my recall—your recall, that is. You'd better get in touch with them and tell them what happened."

"I'll do that. Will you need any help in departing from Earth?"

Karn's eye-slits narrowed contemptuously. "I'm capable of getting back to my own world-line, thanks. It's not that hard to retrace my steps. And then I can continue my work."

"Continuing the job of bottling Earth up?"

"In my world-line," Karn said with a trace of impatience, "the preservation of Hethivar is more important to us than the coddling of Earthers. Go ahead and be altruistic—or asinine; same thing. Luckily, my world-line doesn't have to face the consequences of your actions." He chuckled. "In fact, strictly speaking, you don't even exist."

The other said testily, "May I remind you that at the moment we're both in *my* world-line—and therefore you're the nonexistent one?"

"I'll grant the point," Karn said reluctantly. "But soon I'll be back in my own continuum—the one in which I negotiated the Treaty of Düsseldorf. The one in which the Hethivarian Network will endure for eternity to come, untroubled by Earthers."

"I wish you luck," the other said dryly, and was gone.

What had happened to Karn was humiliating and annoying, but not irremediable. He had been guilty of hasty calculating, that was all; nullspace has infinite exits, and

he had chosen the exit adjoining his own. Exploring probability-worlds was something Karn preferred to leave to
philosophers, poets, and other dreamers; he stuck to solid
reality, the one *real* world-line. All the others were mere
phantoms—including, he thought in relief, the one he had
just left. Earth satellites and atomics indeed! Nightmare!

He blasted off from the New Jersey meadow immediately, and, carrying each calculation out to a dozen places
this time, retraced his steps, returning the ship to orbit,
then converting to nullspace, finally retranslating back into
what he hoped was his own world-line. He had done the
routine arithmetic with scrupulous care this time. He had
small fear of a second error.

He thought about the *other* Earth, the *other* Karn, as he
expertly guided his ship toward Earth a second time.
Karn was no narrow fool; he could understand altruism—
but not suicidal altruism. It was incredible to hear someone
with his own name and identity declaring solemnly and
with a straight face that the proper thing to do was to *help*
Earth attain space.

It was fantastic. But, Karn thought, that was what made
probability-worlds, after all. Now, in *this* world-line, in the
real universe—

He brought the ship down toward Earth and was relieved to see no orbital satellites whirling round the planet.
And his radiation detectors picked up no evidence of
nuclear explosions; the particle count was comfortably
normal for a world that had not yet learned to harness the
power of the atom—for a world that never would learn to
harness it.

Karn felt warm relief. This was the world of the Treaty
of Düsseldorf, at least.

Calmly and confidently, he guided the ship through the

upper atmospheric levels, down toward the same pleasantly green New Jersey meadow he had used for a landing area in that other world, the world he now wanted to forget. He landed under scramblers once again; there was quite possibly no need for them, but Karn had always been cautious and now was doubly so.

He noted the time of landing in his records and prepared to leave the ship. Suddenly he sensed another intelligence nearby. For a wild instant he thought it was another Hethivarian, that he had blundered once again and landed in yet another world-line than his own. But he calmed himself and realized that this was definitely alien, definitely an Earther—

Entering the ship that was supposed to be undetectable by any method save neutrino-detector.

The Earther took form to Karn's left, against the inner wall of the ship. He was of medium height, stocky, with untidy reddish hair and course features. Shocked, Karn was caught midway between his own physical form and the Earthbody he adopted when dealing with the Earther. The Hethivarian completed the change numbly, aghast at the presence of the Earther inside his ship.

"You didn't need to change shapes," the Earther said mildly. "I can see you perfectly well as you really are. Short and squat, with wavy tendrils on your face, and that big eye in the middle of your skull—"

"How did you get in here?" Karn whispered hoarsely.

"Through the wall, of course. Haven't you ever heard of intermolecular penetration? It's a matter of judging the individual magnetic moments, and pushing aside the—"

"Never mind the explanation," Karn said weakly. "I know how it's done. But I didn't know Earthers could autokineticize."

"We haven't been doing it long. I left the Institute five years ago, and I was in the first graduating class. My name is Henrichs, by the way. Are you *really* from another star?"

Karn didn't answer. Terror was sweeping through him, threatening to destabilize him. It was all he could do to hang onto the Earthbody he wore, and not slip back to his own form. And he realized dimly that there was no longer any need for maintaining the pretense, that this was an Earther who could see his real identity, who could auto-kineticize, who could enter minds as only a Hethivarian could—

Karn's mind reeled. *It must be another world-line*, he thought frantically. *But that's impossible. I checked everything a dozen times.*

He had to know. His mind reached toward the smiling Earther's—and recoiled.

"You can put up a barrier, too?" Karn asked.

"Of course. Can't you?"

"I—will you let me enter your mind?" Karn asked.

"What for?"

"I want to find out—find out what universe I'm in," he said in a weak, tired voice.

The Earther lifted the barrier. A moment later, Karn wished he hadn't.

He saw the history of Earth laid out neatly for him in the Earther's mind, as neatly as it had been put in via some history course long before. The course of events followed expectation; with a touch of smugness Karn saw that the Treaty of Düsseldorf *had* existed in this world.

The World War had come to a conclusion in 1916. Karn's work had been successful; the pressures of war had been removed from Earth. But war, it seemed, was not the only stimulus to development. Karn absorbed the history of the years after 1916 with steadily mounting disbelief.

The Earthers had settled down to lives of peaceful, quiet contemplation. There had been many technological advances, of course: radio had become a commercially practicable affair early in the 1920s, aviation had been improved, medicine had taken some steps forward. But there was none of the skyrocketing technological achievement of that other world, the one of the Earth satellite programs and atomic power. Atomics was only a hazy concept in the back of the Earther's mind.

But—behind their national barriers, now safeguarded by the just and wise treaty—these Earthers had developed other skills. Mental skills. Someone named Chalmers had developed the techniques of autokinetics; someone named Resslin had perfected direct communication. And—Karn was appalled—these Earthers seemed to have carried the skills of teleportation to heights undreamed-of even in the Hethivarian Network, which had practiced the power for centuries. On Hethivar, no one even considered an autokinetic jaunt greater than a single planetary diameter—while these Earthers seemed to have made trips all throughout their own solar system in the past few years.

Was the technique different? Or did these Earthers use the same method, but manage it more efficiently, so that they could teleport greater distances? Karn probed deeper. The technique was the same.

That meant—

"You haven't answered my question," Henrichs said. "Do you really come from another star? We've never really tried hopping as far as even Alpha Centauri yet, but if there's life out there—"

Karn shuddered. It took weeks for him to make the trip from Hethivar to Earth by nullspace drive. And this Earther was talking about an instantaneous autokinetic hop! Inconceivable!

"I'd like to know the name of your star," Henrichs persisted. "Maybe we can visit it someday. We're just at the beginning of this thing, you know, but there's never any telling how far we can travel."

Karn felt the Earther probing at his mind, seeking to know the location of the Hethivarian Network. In sudden terror he slammed down the barrier, but it was too little and too late; he felt the Earther pounce on the information.

"No, you can't—"

Karn let his words die away. The Earther was gone.

Karn left Earth several minutes later, sending a radio message ahead to Hethivar that he was returning with very serious news. And very serious it was, indeed.

His manipulations of 1916 had worked out well—too well. Much too well. He had throttled Terran technology so splendidly that their innate drive had forced them to a breakthrough in another, and even more dangerous, field.

Teleportation for billions of miles. Unstoppable entry into ships supposedly invisible. Mental barriers that could not be broken. The thought of what these Earthers had accomplished in a few years' time chilled him—especially when he thought of the years that lay ahead.

He fell into morbid brooding on the return voyage. He realized now that it had been futile to attempt to manipulate the Earthers at all. In that other probability world, his alter ego had conceded the futility of holding the Earthers back, and instead was encouraging them, leading them on to the normal mechanical conquest of space.

Karn and his world had tried a different method, and

succeeded so well that they had perhaps hastened their own downfall by centuries. He pictured a cosmos full of these Terrans, jaunting from world to world while the Hethivarians lumbered along in clumsy nullspace ships—

It took six weeks for him to reach his home world again. From fifty thousand miles up it looked magnificent; he thrilled at the sight of the sweeping pastel-shaded towers standing nobly in the red-and-gold sunslight of midafternoon. He thumbed for direct contact with the Planners. At this distance, telepathy was impossible for him; he would have to radio.

Adric answered. "About time we heard from you, Karn."

"A thousand pardons, Esteemed One. But the news I bring—frightful! Despite our best attempt at holding them back, the Earthers have reached space anyway." Karn scowled glumly. He and all his people had failed. But had the task been possible in the first place? Perhaps the Earthers, driven by some force beyond all logic, could not *have* been held back. Trying to stop them was like attempting to hold back the sea with a toothpick. "They've developed some form of autokinetics that lets them travel huge distances," Karn went on. "I greatly fear—"

Adric interrupted acidly. "Karn, you blitherer, shut up and bring your ship down to land!"

"Esteemed One, I hope you don't blame *me* for—"

"I'm not blaming anyone for what happened," Adric said. The Noble Planner sounded tired, weary, defeated. "But what you're telling me isn't any news. I know all about it."

"You know—"

"Yes," the Planner said. "The first Terran ambassador

showed up here five weeks ago. He didn't need a ship to get here." In an expressionless voice the highest lord of the Hethivarian Network said, "We signed a Treaty of Friendship with the Earthers weeks ago. We signed it on *their* terms."

The Shadow of Wings

••—➤◉➤—••

THE CHILDREN came running toward him, laughing and shouting, up from the lakeside to the spot on the grassy hill where he lay reading; and as Dr. John Donaldson saw what was clutched in the hand of his youngest son, he felt an involuntary tremor of disgust.

"Look, John! Look what Paul caught!" That was his oldest, Joanne. She was nine, a brunette rapidly growing tan on this vacation trip. Behind her came David, eight, fair-haired and lobster-skinned, and in the rear was Paul, the six-year-old, out of breath and gripping in his still pudgy hand a small green frog.

Donaldson shoved his book—Haley, *Studies in Morphological Linguistics*—to one side and sat up. Paul thrust the frog almost into his face. "I saw it hop, John—and I caught it!" He pantomimed the catch with his free hand.

"I saw him do it," affirmed David.

The frog's head projected between thumb and first finger; two skinny webbed feet dangled free at the other end of Paul's hand, while the middle of the unfortunate batrachian was no doubt being painfully compressed by the small clammy hand. Donaldson felt pleased by Paul's display of coordination, unusual for a six-year-old. But at the same time he wished the boy would take the poor frog back to the lake and let it go.

"Paul," he started to say, "you really ought to—"

The direct-wave phone at the far end of the blanket bleeped, indicating that Martha, back at the bungalow, was calling.

"It's Mommy," Joanne said. Somehow they had never cared to call her by her first name, as they did him. "See what she wants, John."

Donaldson sprawled forward and activated the phone. "Martha?"

"John, there's a phone call for you from Washington. I told them you were down by the lake, but they say it's important and they'll hold on."

Donaldson frowned. "Who from Washington?"

"Caldwell, he said. Bureau of Extraterrestrial Affairs. Said it was urgent."

Sighing, Donaldson said, "Okay. I'm coming."

He looked at Joanne and said, as if she hadn't heard the conversation at all, "There's a call for me and I have to go to the cottage to take it. Make sure your brothers don't go into the water while I'm gone. And see that Paul lets that confounded frog go."

Picking up his book, he levered himself to his feet and set out for the phone in the bungalow at a brisk trot.

Caldwell's voice was crisp and efficient and not at all

apologetic as he said, "I'm sorry to have to interrupt you during your vacation, Dr. Donaldson. But it's an urgent matter and they tell us you're the man who can help us."

"Perhaps I am. Just exactly what is it you want?"

"Check me if I'm wrong on the background. You're professor of linguistics at Columbia, a student of the Kethlani languages, and author of a study of Kethlani linguistics published in 2087."

"Yes, yes, that's all correct. But—"

"Dr. Donaldson, we've captured a live Kethlan. He entered the System in a small ship and one of our patrol vessels grappled him in, ship and all. We've got him here in Washington and we want you to come talk to him."

For an instant Donaldson was too stunned to react. A live Kethlan? That was like saying, "We've found a live Sumerian," or, "We've found a live Etruscan."

The Kethlani languages were precise, neat, and utterly dead. At one time in the immeasurable past the Kethlani had visited the Solar System. They had left records of their visit on Mars and Venus, in two languages. One of the languages was translatable, because the Martians had translated it into their own, and the Martian language was still spoken as it had been a hundred thousand years before.

Donaldson had obtained his doctorate with what was hailed as a brilliant Rosetta-stone–type analysis of the Kethlani language. But a *live* Kethlan? Why—

After a moment he realized he was staring stupidly at his unevenly tanned face in the mirror above the phone cabinet, and that the man on the other end of the wire was making impatient noises.

Slowly he said, "I can be in Washington this afternoon, I guess. Give me some time to pack up my things. You won't want me for long, will you?"

"Until we're through talking to the Kethlan," Caldwell said.

"All right," Donaldson said. "I can take a vacation any time. Kethlani don't come along that often."

He hung up and peered at his face in the mirror. He had curly reddish hair once, but fifteen years of the academic life had worn his forehead bare. His eyes were mild, his nose narrow and unemphatic, his lips thin and pale. As he studied himself, he did not think he looked very impressive. He looked professorial. That was to be expected.

"Well?" Martha asked.

Donaldson shrugged. "They captured some kind of alien spaceship with a live one aboard. And it seems I'm the only person who can speak the language. They want me right away."

"You're going?"

"Of course. It shouldn't take more than a few days. You can manage with the children by yourself, can't you? I mean—"

She smiled faintly, walked around behind him, and kneaded the muscle of his sun-reddened back in an affectionate gesture. "I know better than to argue," she said. "We can take a vacation next year."

He swiveled his left hand behind his back, caught her hand, and squeezed it fondly. He knew she would never object. After all, his happiness was her happiness—and he was never happier than when working in his chosen field. The phone call today would probably lead to all sorts of unwanted and unneeded publicity for him. But it would also bring him academic success, and there was no denying the genuine thrill of finding out how accurate his guesses about Kethlani pronunciation were.

"You'd better go down to the lake and get the children," he said. "I'll want to say good-by before I leave."

They had the ship locked in a stasis field in the basement of the Bureau of ET Affairs Building, on Constitution Avenue just across from the National Academy of Sciences. The great room looked like nothing so much as a crypt, Donaldson thought as he entered. Beam projectors were mounted around the walls, focusing a golden glow on the ship. Caught in the field, the ship hovered in midair, a slim, strange-looking torpedolike object about forty feet long and ten feet across the thickest place. A tingle rippled up Donaldson's spine as he saw the Kethlani cursives painted in blue along the hull. He translated them reflexively: *Bringer of Friendship.*

"That's how we knew it was a Kethlani ship," Caldwell said, at his side. He was a small, intense man who hardly reached Donaldson's shoulder; he was associate director of the bureau, and in his superior's absence he was running the show.

Donaldson indicated the projectors. "How come the gadgetry? Couldn't you just sit the ship on the floor instead of floating it that way?"

"That ship's heavy," Caldwell said. "Might crack the floor. Anyway, it's easier to maneuver this way. We can raise or lower the ship, turn it, float it in or out of the door."

"I see," Donaldson said. "And you say there's a live Kethlan in there?"

Caldwell nodded. He jerked a thumb toward a miniature broadcasting station at the far end of the big room. "We've been in contact with him. He talks to us and we talk to him. But we don't understand a damned bit of it, of course. You want to try?"

Donaldson shook his head up and down in a tense affirmative. Caldwell led him down to the radio set, where an eager-looking young man in military uniform sat making adjustments.

Caldwell said, "This is Dr. Donaldson of Columbia. He wrote the definitive book on Kethlani languages. He wants to talk to our friend in there."

A microphone was thrust into Donaldson's hands. He looked at it blankly, then at the pink face of the uniformed man, then at the ship. The inscription was in Kethlani "A" language, for which Donaldson was grateful. There were two Kethlani languages, highly dissimilar, which he labeled A and B. He knew his way around in A well enough, but his mastery of Kethlani B was still exceedingly imperfect.

"How do I use this thing?"

"You push the button on the handle, and talk. That's all. The Kethlan can hear you. Anything he says will be picked up here." He indicated a tape recorder and a speaker on the table.

Donaldson jabbed down on the button, and, feeling a strange sense of disorientation, uttered two words in greeting in Kethlani A.

The pronunciation, of course, was sheer guesswork. Donaldson had worked out what was to him a convincing Kethlani phonetic system, but whether that bore any relation to fact remained to be seen.

He waited a moment. Then the speaker emitted a series of harsh, unfamiliar sounds—and, buried in them like gems in a kitchen midden, Donaldson detected familiar-sounding words.

"Speak slowly," he said in Kethlani A. "I . . . have only a few words."

The reply came about ten seconds later, in more measured accents. "How . . . do . . . you . . . speak our language?"

Donaldson fumbled in his small vocabulary for some way of explaining that he had studied Kethlani documents left behind on Mars centuries earlier, and compared them with their understandable Martian translations until he had pried some sense out of them.

He glimpsed the pale, sweat-beaded faces of the ET men around him; they were mystified, wondering what he was saying to the alien but not daring to interrupt. Donaldson felt a flash of pity for them. Until today the bureau had concerned itself with petty things: import of Martian antiquities, study visas for Venus, and the like. Now, suddenly, they found themselves staring at an extrasolar spaceship, and all the giant problems that entailed.

"Find out why he came to the Solar System," Caldwell whispered.

"I'm trying to," Donaldson murmured with some irritation. He said in Kethlani, "You have made a long journey."

"Yes . . . and alone."

"Why have you come?"

There was a moment of silence; Donaldson waited, feeling tension of crackling intensity starting to build within him. The unreality of the situation obsessed him. He had been fondly confident that he would never have the opportunity to speak actual Kethlani, and that confidence was being shattered.

Finally: "I . . . have come . . . why?"

The inversion was grammatically correct. "Yes," Donaldson said. "Why?"

Another long pause. Then the alien said something which Donaldson did not immediately understand. He asked for a repeat.

It made little sense—but, of course, his Kethlani vocabulary was a shallow one, and he had additional difficulty in comprehending because he had made some mistakes in interpreting vowel values when constructing his Kethlani phonetics.

But the repeat came sharp and clear, and there was no mistaking it:

"I do . . . do not like to talk this way. Come inside my ship and we will talk there."

"What's he saying?" Caldwell prodded.

Shaken, Donaldson let the mike dangle from limp fingers. "He—he says he wants me to come inside the ship. He doesn't like long-distance conversations."

Caldwell turned at a right angle and said to a waiting assistant, "All right. Have Mathews reverse the stasis field and lower the ship. We're going to give the Kethlan some company."

Donaldson blinked. "Company? You mean you're sending me in there?"

"I sure as hell do mean that. The Kethlan said it's the only way he'd talk, didn't he? And that's what you're here for. To talk to him. So why shouldn't you go in there, eh?"

"Well—look, Caldwell, suppose it isn't safe?"

"If I thought it was risky, I wouldn't send you in," Caldwell said blandly.

Donaldson shook his head. "But look—I don't want to seem cowardly, but I've got three children to think about. I'm not happy about facing an alien being inside his own ship, if you get me."

"I get you," Caldwell said tiredly. "All right. You want to go home? You want to call the whole business off right here and now?"

"Of course not. But—"

"But then you'll have to go in."

"How will I be able to breathe?"

"The alien air is close enough to our own. He's used to more carbon dioxide and less oxygen, but he can handle our air. There's no problem. And no risk. We had a man in there yesterday when the Kethlan opened the outer lock. You won't be in any physical danger. The alien won't bother you."

"I hope not," Donaldson said. He felt hesitant about it; he hadn't bargained on going inside any extrasolar spaceships. But they were clustered impatiently around him, waiting to send him inside, and he didn't seem to have much choice. . . . He sensed a certain contempt for him on their faces already. He didn't want to increase their distaste.

"Will you go in?" Caldwell asked.

"All right. All right. Yes. I'll go in."

Nervously Donaldson picked up the microphone and clamped a cold finger over the control button.

"Open your lock," he said to the alien being. "I'm coming inside."

There was a moment's delay while the stasis field projectors were reversed, lowering the ship gently to floor level. As soon as it touched, a panel in the gleaming golden side of the ship rolled smoothly open, revealing an inner panel.

Donaldson moistened his lips, handed the microphone to Caldwell and walked uncertainly forward. He reached the lip of the air lock, stepped over it and into the ship. Immediately the door rolled shut behind him, closing him into a chamber about seven feet high and four feet wide, bordered in front and back by the outer and inner doors of the lock.

He waited. Had he been claustrophobic he would have been hysterical by now. *But I never would have come in here in the first place then*, he thought.

He waited. More than a minute passed; then, finally, the blank wall before him rolled aside, and the ship was open to him at last. He entered.

At first it seemed to him the interior was totally dark. Gradually, his retinal rods conveyed a little information.

A dim light flickered at one end of the narrow, tubular ship. He could make out a few things: rows of reinforcing struts circling the ship at regularly spaced distances; a kind of control panel with quite thoroughly alien-looking instruments on it; a large chamber at one end which might be used for storage of food.

But where's the alien? Donaldson wondered.

He turned, slowly, through a three-hundred-sixty-degree rotation, squinting in the dimness. A sort of mist hung before his eyes; the alien's exhalation, perhaps. But he saw no sign of the Kethlan. There was a sweetish, musky odor in the ship, unpleasant though not unbearable.

"Everything okay?" Caldwell's voice said in his earphones.

"So far. But I can't find the alien. It's damnably dark in here."

"Look up," Caldwell advised. "You'll find him. Took our man a while, too, yesterday."

Puzzled, Donaldson raised his head and stared into the gloom-shrouded rafters of the ship, wondering what he was supposed to see. In Kethlani he said loudly, "Where are you? I see you not."

"I am here," came the harsh voice, from above.

Donaldson looked. Then he backed away, double-taking, and looked again.

A great shaggy thing hung head down against the roof

of the ship. Staring intently, Donaldson made out a blunt, piggish face with flattened nostrils and huge flaring ears; the eyes, bright yellow but incredibly tiny, glittered with the unmistakable light of intelligence. He saw a body about the size of a man, covered with darkish thick fur and terminating in two short, thick, powerful-looking legs. As he watched the Kethlan shivered and stretched forth its vast leathery wings. In the darkness, Donaldson could see the corded muscular arm in the wing, and the very human-looking fingers which sprouted from the uppermost part of the wing.

Violent disgust rose in him, compounded from his own general dislike for animals and from the half-remembered Transylvanian folktales that formed part of every child's heritage. He felt sick; he controlled himself only by remembering that he was in essence an ambassador, and any sickness would have disastrous consequences for him and for Earth. He dared not offend the Kethlan.

My God, he thought. *An intelligent bat!*

He managed to stammer out the words for greeting, and the alien responded. Donaldson, looking away, saw the elongated shadow of wings cast across the ship by the faint light at the other end. He felt weak, wobbly-legged; he wanted desperately to dash through the now-closed air lock. But he forced himself to recover balance. He had a job to do.

"I did not expect you to know Kethlani," the alien said. "It makes my job much less difficult."

"And your job is—?"

"To bring friendship from my people to yours. To link our worlds in brotherhood."

The last concept was a little muddy to Donaldson; the literal translation he made mentally was *children-of-one-*

cave, but some questioning eventually brought over the concept of brotherhood.

His eyes were growing more accustomed to the lighting now, and he could see the Kethlan fairly well. An ugly brute, no doubt of it—but probably I look just as bad to him, he thought. The creature's wingspread was perhaps seven or eight feet. Donaldson tried to picture a world of the beasts, skies thick with leather-winged commuters on their way to work.

Evolution had made numerous modifications in the bat structure, Donaldson saw. The brain, of course; and the extra fingers, aside from the ones which the wings had sprouted. The eyes looked weak, in typical fashion, but probably there was compensation by way of keen auditory senses.

Donaldson said, "Where is your world?"

"Far from here. It—"

The rest of the answer was unintelligible to Donaldson. He felt savage impatience with his own limited vocabulary; he wished he had worked just a little harder on translating the Syrtis Major documents. Well, it was too late for that now, of course.

Caldwell cut in suddenly from outside. "Well? We're picking up all the jabber. What's all the talk about?"

"Can't you wait till I'm finished?" Donaldson snapped. Then, repenting, he said: "Sorry. Guess I'm jumpy. Seems he's an ambassador from his people, trying to establish friendly relations with us. At least, I think so. I'll tell you more when I know something about it."

Slowly, in fits and starts, the story emerged. Frequently Donaldson had to ask the Kethlan to stop and double back while he puzzled over a word. He had no way of recording any of the new words he was learning, but he had always had a good memory, and he simply tucked them away.

The Kethlani had visited the Solar System many years ago. Donaldson was unable to translate the actual figure, but it sounded like a lot. At that time the Martians were at the peak of their civilization, and Earth was just an untamed wilderness populated by naked primates. The Kethlan wryly admitted that they had written off Earth as a potential place of civilization because a study of the bat population of Earth had proved unpromising. They had never expected the primates to evolve this way.

But now they had returned, thousands of years later. Mars was bleak and its civilization decayed, but the third world had unexpectedly attained a high degree of culture and was welcome to embrace the Kethlani worlds in friendship and amity.

"How many worlds do you inhabit?"

The Kethlan counted to fifteen, by ones. "There are many others we do not inhabit, but simply maintain friendly relations with. Yours would be one, we hope."

The conversation seemed to dwindle to a halt. Donaldson had run out of questions to ask, and he was exhausted by the hour-long strain of conversing in an alien language, under these conditions, within a cramped ship, talking to a creature whose physical appearance filled him with loathing and fear.

His head throbbed. His stomach was knotted in pain and sweat made his clothes cling clammily to his body. He started to grope for ways to terminate the interview; then an idea struck him.

He quoted a fragment of a document written in pure Kethlani B.

There was an instant of stunned silence; then the alien

asked in tones of unmistakable suspicion, "Where did you learn that language?"

"I haven't really learned it. I just know a few words."

He explained that he had found examples of both Kethlani A and Kethlani B along with their Martian equivalents; he had worked fairly comprehensively on the A language, but had only begun to explore the B recently.

The Kethlan seemed to accept that. Then it said: "That is not a Kethlani language."

Surprised, Donaldson uttered the interrogative expletive.

The Kethlan said, "It is the language of our greatest enemies, our rivals, our bitter foes. It is the Thygnor tongue."

"But—why did we find your language and the other side by side, then?"

After a long pause the alien said, "Once Thygnor and Kethlan were friends. Long age we conducted a joint expedition to this sector of space. Long ago, before the rivalry sprang up. But now"— the alien took on a sorrowful inflection—"now we are enemies."

That explained a great many things, Donaldson realized. The differences between Kethlani A and Kethlani B had been too great for it to seem as if one race spoke both of them. But a joint expedition—that made it understandable.

"Some day, perhaps, the Thygnor will visit your world. But by then you will be on guard against them."

"What do they look like?"

The alien described them, and Donaldson listened and was revolted. As far as he could understand, they were giant intelligent toads, standing erect, amphibian but warm-blooded, vile-smelling, their bodies exuding a nauseous thick secretion.

Giant toads, bats, the lizards of Mars—evidently the primate monopoly of intelligence was confined solely to Earth, Donaldson realized. It was a humbling thought. His face wrinkled in displeasure at the mental image of the toad people the Kethlan had created for him, as he recalled the harmless little frog Paul had captured by the lake.

He spoke in English, attracting Caldwell's attention, and explained the situation.

"He wants me to swear brotherhood with him. He also says there's another intelligent race with interstellar travel —toads, no less—and that they're likely to pay us a visit some day, too. What should I do?"

"Go ahead and swear brotherhood," Caldwell said after a brief pause. "It can't hurt. We can always unswear it later, if we like. Say we had our fingers crossed while we were doing it, or something. Then when the frogs get here, we can find out which bunch is better for us to be in league with."

The cynicism of the reply annoyed Donaldson, but it was not his place to raise any objections. He said to the alien, "I am prepared to pledge brotherhood between Earth and the Kethlan worlds."

The Kethlan fluttered suddenly down from its perch with a rustle of great wings, and stood facing Donaldson, tucking its wings around its thick, shaggy body. Alarmed, Donaldson stepped back.

The alien said reassuringly, "The way we pledge is by direct physical embrace, symbolizing harmony and friendship across the cosmos." He unfurled his wings. "Come close to me."

No! Donaldson shrieked inwardly, as the mighty wings

rose high and wrapped themselves about him. *Go away! Don't touch me!* He could smell the sweet, musky smell of the alien, feel its furry warmth, hear the mighty heart pounding, pounding in that massive rib cage. . . .

Revulsion dizzied him. He forced himself to wrap his arms around the barrel of a body while the wings blanketed him, and they stood that way for a moment, locked in a tight embrace.

At length the alien released him. "Now we are friends. It is only the beginning of a long and fruitful relationship between our peoples. I hope to speak with you again before long."

It was a dismissal. On watery legs Donaldson tottered forward toward the opening air lock, pausing only to mutter a word of farewell before he stumbled through and out into the arms of the waiting men outside.

"Well?" Caldwell demanded. "What happened? Did you swear brotherhood?"

"Yes," Donaldson said wearily. "I swore." The stench of the alien clung to him, sweet in his nostrils. It was as though throbbing wings still enfolded him. "I'm leaving now," he said. "I still have a little of my vacation left. I want to take it."

He gulped a drink someone handed him. He was shaking and gray-faced, but the effect of the embrace was wearing off. *Only an irrational phobia*, he told himself. *I shouldn't be reacting this way.*

But already he was beginning to forget the embrace of the Kethlan, and the rationalization did him no good. A new and more dreadful thought was beginning to develop within him.

He was the only Terrestrial expert on Kethlani B, too —the Thygnor tongue. And some day, perhaps soon, the Thygnor were going to come to Earth, and Caldwell was going to impress him into service as an interpreter again.

He wondered how the toad people pledged eternal brotherhood.

Absolutely Inflexible

···━●◉●━···

THE DETECTOR over in one corner of Mahler's little office gleamed a soft red. He indicated it with a weary gesture of his hand to the sad-eyed time-jumper who sat slouched glumly across the desk from him, looking cramped and uncomfortable in the bulky spacesuit he was compelled to wear.

"You see," Mahler said, tapping his desk. "They've just found another one. We're constantly bombarded with you people. When you get to the Moon, you'll find a whole Dome full of them. I've sent over four thousand there myself since I took over the bureau. And that was eight years ago—in 2776. An average of five hundred a year. Hardly a day goes by without someone dropping in on us."

"And not one has been set free," the time-jumper said. "Every time-traveler who's come here has been packed off to the Moon immediately. Every one."

"Every one," Mahler said. He peered through the thick shielding, trying to see what sort of man was hidden inside the spacesuit. Mahler often wondered about the men he condemned so easily to the Moon. This one was small of stature, with wispy locks of white hair pasted to his high forehead by perspiration. Evidently he had been a scientist, a respected man of his time, perhaps a happy father (although very few of the time-jumpers were family men). Perhaps he possessed some bit of scientific knowledge that would be invaluable to the twenty-eighth century; perhaps not. It did not matter. Like all the rest, he would have to be sent to the Moon, to live out his remaining days under the grueling, primitive conditions of the Dome.

"Don't you think that's a little cruel?" the other asked. "I came here with no malice, no intent to harm whatsoever. I'm simply a scientific observer from the past. Driven by curiosity, I took the Jump. I never expected that I'd be walking into life imprisonment."

"I'm sorry," Mahler said, getting up. He decided to end the interview; he had to get rid of this jumper because there was another coming right up. Some days they came thick and fast, and this looked like one of them. But the efficient mechanical tracers never missed one.

"But can't I live on Earth and stay in this spacesuit?" the time-jumper asked, panicky now that he saw his interview with Mahler was coming to an end. "That way I'd be sealed off from contact at all times."

"Please don't make this any harder for me," Mahler said. "I've explained to you why we must be absolutely inflexible about this. There cannot—must not—be any exceptions. It's two centuries since last there was any occurrence of disease on Earth. In all this time we've lost most of the resistance acquired over the previous countless generations of disease. I'm risking my life coming so close to you, even with the spacesuit sealing you off."

Mahler signaled to the tall, powerful guards waiting in the corridor, grim in the casings that protected them from infection. This was always the worst moment.

"Look," Mahler said, frowning with impatience. "You're a walking death trap. You probably carry enough disease germs to kill half the world. Even a cold, a common cold, would wipe out millions now. Resistance to disease has simply vanished over the past two centuries; it isn't needed, with all diseases conquered. But you time-travelers show up loaded with potentialities for all the diseases the world used to have. And we can't risk having you stay here with them."

"But I'd—"

"I know. You'd swear by all that's holy to you or to me that you'd never leave the confines of the spacesuit. Sorry. The word of the most honorable man doesn't carry any weight against the safety of the lives of Earth's billions. We can't take the slightest risk by letting you stay on Earth. It's unfair, it's cruel, it's everything else. You had no idea you would walk into something like this. Well, it's too bad for you. But you knew you were going on a one-way trip to the future, and you're subject to whatever that future wants to do with you, since there's no way of getting back."

Mahler began to tidy up the papers on his desk in a way that signaled finality. "I'm terribly sorry, but you'll just have to see our way of thinking about it. We're frightened to death at your very presence here. We can't allow you to roam Earth, even in a spacesuit. No; there's nothing for you but the Moon. I have to be absolutely inflexible. Take him away," he said, gesturing to the guards. They advanced on the little man and began gently to ease him out of Mahler's office.

Mahler sank gratefully into the pneumochair and sprayed his throat with laryngogel. These long speeches always left him feeling exhausted, his throat feeling raw and scraped. Someday I'll get throat cancer from all this talking, Mahler thought. And that'll mean the nuisance of an operation. But if I don't do this job, someone else will have to.

Mahler heard the protesting screams of the time-jumper impassively. In the beginning he had been ready to resign when he first witnessed the inevitable frenzied reaction of jumper after jumper as the guards dragged them away, but eight years had hardened him.

They had given him the job because he was hard, in the first place. It was a job that called for a hard man. Condrin, his predecessor, had not been the same sort of man Mahler was, and for that reason Condrin was now himself on the Moon. He had weakened after heading the Bureau for a year and had let a jumper go; the jumper had promised to secrete himself at the tip of Antarctica, and Condrin, thinking that Antarctica was as safe as the Moon, had foolishly released him. That was when they called Mahler in. In eight years Mahler had sent four thousand men to the Moon. (The first was the runaway jumper, intercepted in Buenos Aires after he had left a trail of disease down the hemisphere from Appalachia to Argentine Protectorate. The second was Condrin.)

It was getting to be a tiresome job, Mahler thought. But he was proud to hold it. It took a strong man to do what he was doing. He leaned back and awaited the arrival of the next jumper.

The door slid smoothly open as the burly body of Dr. Fournet, the Bureau's chief medical man, broke the photoelectronic beam. Mahler glanced up. Fournet carried a time-rig dangling from one hand.

"Took this away from our latest customer," Fournet said. "He told the medic who examined him that it was a two-way rig, and I thought I'd bring it to show you."

Mahler came to full attention quickly. A two-way rig? Unlikely, he thought. But it would mean the end of the dreary jumper prison on the Moon if it were true. Only how could a two-way rig exist?

He reached out and took it from Fournet. "It seems to be a conventional twenty-fourth century type," he said.

"But notice the extra dial here," Fournet said, pointing. Mahler peered and nodded.

"Yes. It *seems* to be a two-way rig. But how can we test it? And it's not really very probable," Mahler said. "Why should a two-way rig suddenly show up from the twenty-fourth century when no other traveler's had one? We don't even have two-way time-travel ourselves, and our scientists don't think it's possible. Still," he mused, "it's a nice thing to dream about. We'll have to study this a little more closely. But I don't seriously think it'll work. Bring him in, will you?"

As Fournet turned to signal the guards, Mahler asked him, "What's his medical report, by the way?"

"From here to here," Fournet said somberly. "You name it, he's carrying it. Better get him shipped off to the Moon as soon as possible. I won't feel safe until he's off this planet." The big medic waved to the guards.

Mahler smiled. Fournet's overcautiousness was proverbial in the Bureau. Even if a jumper were to show up completely free from disease, Fournet would probably insist that he was carrying everything from asthma to leprosy.

The guards brought the jumper into Mahler's office. He

was fairly tall, Mahler saw, and young. It was difficult to see his face clearly through the dim plate of the protective spacesuit all jumpers were compelled to wear, but Mahler could tell that the young time-jumper's face had much of the lean, hard look of Mahler's own. It seemed that the jumper's eyes had widened in surprise as he entered the office, but Mahler was not sure.

"I never dreamed I'd find you here," the jumper said. The transmitter of the spacesuit brought his voice over deeply and resonantly. "Your name is Mahler, isn't it?"

"That's right," Mahler agreed.

"To go all these years—and find you. Talk about improbabilities!"

Mahler ignored him, declining to take up the gambit. He had found it was good practice never to let a captured jumper get the upper hand in conversation. His standard procedure was firmly to explain to the jumper the reasons why it was imperative that he be sent to the Moon, and then send him, as quickly as possible.

"You say this is a two-way time-rig?" Mahler asked, holding up the flimsy-looking piece of equipment.

"That's right," the other agreed. "Works both ways. If you pressed the button, you'd go straight back to 2360 or thereabouts."

"Did you build it?"

"Me? No, hardly," said the jumper. "I found it. It's a long story, and I don't have time to tell it. In fact, if I tried to tell it, I'd only make things ten times worse than they are, if that's possible. No. Let's get this over with, shall we? I know I don't stand much of a chance with you, and I'd just as soon make it quick."

"You know, of course, that this is a world without disease—" Mahler began sonorously.

"And that you think I'm carrying enough germs of different sorts to wipe out the whole world. And therefore you have to be absolutely inflexible with me. I won't try to argue with you. Which way is the Moon?"

Absolutely inflexible. The phrase Mahler had used so many times, the phrase that summed him up so neatly. He chuckled to himself; some of the younger technicians must have tipped the jumper off about the usual procedure, and the jumper was resigned to going peacefully, without bothering to plead. It was just as well.

Absolutely inflexible.

Yes, Mahler thought, the words fit him well. He was becoming a stereotype in the Bureau. Perhaps he was the only Bureau chief who had never relented and let a jumper go. Probably all the others, bowed under the weight of the hordes of curious men flooding in from the past, had finally cracked and taken the risk. But not Mahler; not Absolutely Inflexible Mahler. He knew the deep responsibility that rode on his shoulders, and he had no intention of failing what amounted to a sacred trust. His job was to find the jumpers and get them off Earth as quickly and as efficiently as possible. Every one. It was a task that required unsoftening inflexibility.

"This makes my job much easier," Mahler said. "I'm glad I won't have to convince you of the necessity of my duty."

"Not at all," the other agreed. "I understand. I won't even waste my breath. You have good reasons for what you're doing, and nothing I say can alter them." He turned to the guards. "I'm ready. Take me away."

Mahler gestured to them, and they led the jumper away. Amazed, Mahler watched the retreating figure, studying him until he could no longer be seen.

If they were all like that, Mahler thought.

I could have gotten to like that one. That was a sensible man—one of the few. He knew he was beaten, and he didn't try to argue in the face of absolute necessity. It's too bad he had to go; he's the kind of man I'd like to find more often these days.

But I mustn't feel sympathy, Mahler told himself.

He had performed his job so well so long because he had managed to suppress any sympathy for the unfortunates he had to condemn. Had there been someplace else to send them—back to their own time, preferably—he would have been the first to urge abolition of the Moon prison. But, with no place else to send them, he performed this job efficiently and automatically.

He picked up the jumper's time-rig and examined it. A two-way rig would be the solution, of course. As soon as the jumper arrives, turn him around and send him back. They'd get the idea soon enough. Mahler found himself wishing it were so; he often wondered what the jumpers stranded on the Moon must think of him.

A two-way rig could change the world completely; its implications were staggering. With men able to move with ease backward and forward in time, past, present, and future would blend into one mind-numbing new entity. It was impossible to conceive of the world as it would be, with free passage in either direction.

But even as Mahler fondled the confiscated time-rig he realized something was wrong. In the six centuries since the development of time-travel, no one had yet developed a known two-way rig. And, more important, there were no documented reports of visitors from the future. Presumably, if a two-way rig existed, such visitors would be commonplace.

So the jumper had been lying, Mahler thought with regret. The two-way rig was an impossibility. He had merely been playing a game with his captors. This *couldn't* be a two-way rig, because the past held no record of anyone's going back.

Mahler examined the rig. There were two dials on it, one the conventional forward dial and the other indicating backward travel. Whoever had prepared this hoax had gone to considerable extent to document it. *Why?*

Could it be that the jumper had told the truth? Mahler wished he could somehow test the rig in his hands; there was always that one chance that it might actually work, that he would no longer have to be the rigid dispenser of justice, Absolutely Inflexible Mahler.

He looked at it. As a time machine, it was fairly crude. It made use of the standard distorter pattern, but the dial was the clumsy wide-range twenty-fourth-century one; the vernier system, Mahler reflected, had not been introduced until the twenty-fifth.

Mahler peered closer to read the instruction label. PLACE LEFT HAND HERE, it said. He studied it carefully. The ghost of a thought wandered into his mind; he pushed it aside in horror, but it recurred. It would be so simple. What if—?

No.

But—

PLACE LEFT HAND HERE.

He reached out tentatively with his left hand.

Just a bit—

No.

PLACE LEFT HAND HERE.

He touched his hand gingerly to the indicated place. There was a little crackle of electricity. He let go, quickly, and started to replace the time-rig on his desk when the desk abruptly faded out from under him.

The air was foul and grimy. Mahler wondered what had happened to the conditioner. Then he looked around.

Huge, grotesque buildings raised to the sky. Black, despairing clouds of smoke overhead. The harsh screech of an industrial society.

He was in the middle of an immense city, with streams of people rushing past him on the street at a furious pace. They were all small, stunted creatures, angry-looking, their faces harried, neurotic. It was the same black, frightened expression Mahler had seen so many times on the faces of jumpers escaping to what they hoped might be a more congenial future.

He looked at the time-rig clutched in one hand, and knew what had happened.

The two-way rig.

It meant the end of the Moon prisons. It meant a complete revolution in civilization. But he had no further business back in this age of nightmare. He reached down to activate the time-rig.

Abruptly someone jolted him from behind. The current of the crowd swept him along, as he struggled to regain his control over himself. Suddenly a hand reached out and grabbed the back of his neck.

"Got a card, Hump?"

He whirled to face an ugly, squinting-eyed man in a dull-brown uniform with a row of metallic buttons.

"Hear me? Where's your card, Hump? Talk up or you get Spotted."

Mahler twisted out of the man's grasp and started to jostle his way through the crowd, desiring nothing more than a moment to set the time-rig and get out of this disease-ridden squalid era. As he shoved people out of his way, they shouted angrily at him.

"There's a Hump!" someone called. "Spot him!"

The cry became a roar. "Spot him! Spot him!

Wherever—whenever—he was, it was no place to stay in long. He turned left and went pounding down a side street, and now it was a full-fledged mob that dashed after him, shouting wildly.

"Send for the Crimers!" a deep voice boomed. "They'll Spot him!"

Someone caught up to him, and without looking Mahler reached behind and hit out, hard. He heard a dull grunt of pain, and continued running. The unaccustomed exercise was tiring him rapidly.

An open door beckoned. He stepped inside, finding himself inside a machine store of sorts, and slammed the door shut. They still had manual doors, a remote part of his mind observed coldly.

A salesman came toward him. "Can I help you, sir? The latest models, right here."

"Just leave me alone," Mahler panted, squinting at the time-rig. The salesman watched uncomprehendingly as Mahler fumbled with the little dial.

There was no vernier. He'd have to chance it and hope he hit the right year. The salesman suddenly screamed and came to life, for reasons Mahler would never understand. Mahler averted him and punched the stud viciously.

It was wonderful to step back into the serenity of twenty-eighth-century Appalachia. Small wonder so many time-jumpers come here, Mahler reflected, as he waited for his overworked heart to calm down. Almost anything would be preferable to *then*.

He looked around the quiet street for a Convenience

where he could repair the scratches and bruises he had acquired during his brief stay in the past. They would scarcely be able to recognize him at the Bureau in his present battered condition, with one eye nearly closed, a great livid welt on his cheek, and his clothing hanging in tatters.

He sighted a Convenience and started down the street, pausing at the sound of a familiar soft mechanical whining. He looked around to see one of the low-running mechanical tracers of the Bureau purring up the street toward him, closely followed by the two Bureau guards, clad in their protective casings.

Of course. He had arrived from the past, and the detectors had recorded his arrival, as they would that of any time-traveler. They never missed.

He turned and walked toward the guards. He failed to recognize either one, but this did not surprise him; the Bureau was a vast and wide-ranging organization, and he knew only a handful of the many guards who accompanied the tracers. It was a pleasant relief to see the tracer; the use of tracers had been instituted during his administration, so at least he knew he hadn't returned too early along the time-stream.

"Good to see you," he called to the approaching guards. "I had a little accident in the office."

They ignored him and methodically unpacked a spacesuit from the storage trunk of the mechanical tracer. "Never mind talking," one said. "Get into this."

He paled. "But I'm no jumper," he said. "Hold on a moment, fellows. This is all a mistake. I'm Mahler—head of the Bureau. Your boss."

"Don't play games with us, fellow," the taller guard said, while the other forced the spacesuit down over

Mahler. To his horror, Mahler saw that they did not recognize him at all.

"If you'll just come peacefully and let the Chief explain everything to you, without any trouble—" the short guard said.

"But I *am* the Chief," Mahler protested. "I was examining a two-way time-rig in my office and accidentally sent myself back to the past. Take this thing off me and I'll show you my identification card; that should convince you."

"Look, fellow, we don't want to be convinced of anything. Tell it to the Chief if you want. Now, are you coming, or do we bring you?"

There was no point, Mahler decided, in trying to prove his identity to the clean-faced young medic who examined him at the Bureau office. That would only add more complications, he realized. No; he would wait until he reached the office of the Chief.

He saw now what had happened: Apparently he had landed somewhere in his own future, shortly after his own death. Someone else had taken over the Bureau, and he, Mahler, was forgotten. (Mahler suddenly realized with a shock that at this very moment his ashes were probably reposing in an urn at the Appalachia Crematorium.)

When he got to the Chief of the Bureau, he would simply and calmly explain his identity and ask for permission to go back the ten or twenty or thirty years to the time in which he belonged, and where he could turn the two-way rig over to the proper authorities and resume his life from his point of departure. And when that happened, the jumpers would no longer be sent to the Moon, and there would be no further need for Absolutely Inflexible Mahler.

But, he realized, if I've already done this then why is there still a Bureau now? An uneasy fear began to grow in him.

"Hurry up and finish that report," Mahler told the medic.

"I don't know what the rush is," the medic said. "Unless you like it on the Moon."

"Don't worry about me," Mahler said confidently. "If I told you who I am, you'd think twice about—"

"Is this thing your time-rig?" the medic asked boredly, interrupting.

"Not really. I mean—yes, yes it is," Mahler said. "And be careful with it. It's the world's only two-way rig."

"Really, now?" said the medic. "Two ways, eh?"

"Yes. And if you'll take me in to your Chief—"

"Just a minute. I'd like to show this to the Head Medic."

In a few moments the medic returned. "All right, let's go to the Chief now. I'd advise you not to bother arguing; you can't win. You should have stayed where you came from."

Two guards appeared and jostled Mahler down the familiar corridor to the brightly lit little office where he had spent eight years. Eight years on the other side of the fence.

As he approached the door of what had once been his office, he carefully planned what he would say to his successor. He would explain the accident, demonstrate his identity as Mahler, and request permission to use the two-way rig to return to his own time. The Chief would probably be belligerent at first, then curious, finally amused at the chain of events that had ensnarled Mahler. And, of course, he would let him go, after they had exchanged anecdotes about their job, the job they both held at the same time and across a gap of years. Mahler swore never again to touch a time machine, once he got back. He would let others undergo the huge job of transmitting the jumpers back to their own eras.

He moved forward and broke the photoelectronic beam. The door to the Bureau Chief's office slid open. Behind the desk sat a tall, powerful-looking man, lean, hard.

Me.

Through the dim plate of the spacesuit into which he had been stuffed, Mahler saw the man behind the desk. Himself. Absolutely Inflexible Mahler. The man who had sent four thousand men to the Moon, without exception, in the unbending pursuit of his duty.

And if he's Mahler—

Who am I?

Suddenly Mahler saw the insane circle complete. He recalled the jumper, the firm, deep-voiced, unafraid time-jumper who had arrived claiming to have a two-way rig and who had marched off to the Moon without arguing. Now Mahler knew who that jumper was.

But how did the cycle start? Where did the two-way rig come from in the first place? He had gone to the past to bring it to the present to take it to the past to—

His head swam. There was no way out. He looked at the man behind the desk and began to walk toward him, feeling a wall of circumstance growing around him, while he, in frustration, tried impotently to beat his way out.

It was utterly pointless to argue. Not with Absolutely Inflexible Mahler. It would just be a waste of breath. The wheel had come full circle, and he was as good as on the

Moon. He looked at the man behind the desk with a new, strange light in his eyes.

"I never dreamed I'd find you here," the jumper said. The transmitter of the spacesuit brought his voice over deeply and resonantly.

The Iron Chancellor

······—◉—······

THE CARMICHAELS WERE a pretty plump family, to begin with. Not one of the four of them couldn't stand to shed quite a few pounds. And there happened to be a superspecial on roboservitors at one of the Miracle Mile roboshops—40 percent off on the 2061 model, with adjustable caloric-intake monitors.

Sam Carmichael liked the idea of having his food prepared and served by a robot who would keep one beady eye on the collective family waistline. He squinted speculatively at the glossy display model, absent-mindedly slipped his thumbs beneath his elastobelt to knead his paunch, and said, "How much?"

The salesman flashed a brilliant and probably synthetic grin. "Only two thousand nine hundred and ninety-five, sir. That includes free service contract for the first five years.

Only two hundred credits down and up to forty months to pay."

Carmichael frowned, thinking of his bank balance. Then he thought of his wife's figure, and of his daughter's endless yammering about her need to diet. Besides, Jemima, their old robocook, was shabby and gear-stripped, and made a miserable showing when other company executives visited them for dinner.

"I'll take it," he said.

"Care to trade in your old robocook, sir? Liberal trade-in allowances—"

"I have a '43 Madison." Carmichael wondered if he should mention its bad arm libration and serious fuelfeed overflow, but decided that would be carrying candidness too far.

"Well—ah—I guess we could allow you fifty credits on a '43, sir. Seventy-five, maybe, if the recipe bank is still in good condition."

"Excellent condition." That part was honest—the family had never let even one recipe wear out. "You could send a man down to look her over."

"Oh, no need to do that, sir. We'll take your word. Seventy-five, then? And delivery of the new model by this evening?"

"Done," Carmichael said. He was glad to get the pathetic old '43 out of the house at any cost.

He signed the purchase order cheerfully, pocketed the facsim and handed over ten crisp twenty-credit vouchers. He could almost feel the roll of fat melting from him now, as he eyed the magnificent '61 reboservitor that would shortly be his.

The time was only 1810 hours when he left the shop, got into his car, and punched out coordinates for home.

The whole transaction had taken less than ten minutes. Carmichael, a second-level executive at Normandy Trust, prided himself both on his good business sense and his ability to come quickly to a firm decision.

Fifteen minutes later, his car deposited him at the front entrance of their totally detached self-powered suburban home in the fashionable Westley subdivision. The car obediently took itself around back to the garage, while Carmichael stood in the scanner field until the door opened. Clyde, the robutler, came scuttling hastily up, took his hat and cloak, and handed him a martini.

Carmichael beamed appreciatively. "Well done, thou good and faithful servant!"

He took a healthy sip and headed toward the living room to greet his wife, son, and daughter. Pleasant gin-induced warmth filtered through him. The robutler was ancient and due for replacement as soon as the budget could stand the charge, but Carmichael realized he would miss the clanking old heap.

"You're late, dear," Ethel Carmichael said as he appeared. "Dinner's been ready for ten minutes. Jemima's so annoyed her cathodes are clicking."

"Jemima's cathodes fail to interest me," Carmichael said evenly. "Good evening, dear. Myra. Joey. I'm late because I stopped off at Marhew's on my way home."

His son blinked. "The robot place, Dad?"

"Precisely. I bought a '61 roboservitor to replace old Jemima and her sputtering cathodes. The new model has," Carmichael added, eyeing his son's adolescent bulkiness and the rather more-than-ample figures of his wife and daughter, "some very special attachments."

They dined well that night, on Jemima's favorite Tuesday dinner menu—shrimp cocktail, fumet of gumbo chervil, breast of chicken with creamed potatoes and asparagus, delicious plum tarts for dessert, and coffee. Carmichael felt pleasantly bloated when he had finished, and gestured to Clyde for a snifter of his favorite after-dinner digestive aid, VSOP cognac. He leaned back, warm, replete, able easily to ignore the blustery November winds outside.

A pleasing electroluminescence suffused the dining room with pink—this year the experts thought pink improved digestion—and the heating filaments embedded in the wall glowed cozily as they delivered the BTUs. This was the hour for relaxation in the Carmichael household.

"Dad," Joey began hesitantly, "about that canoe trip next weekend—"

Carmichael folded his hands across his stomach and nodded. "You can go, I suppose. Only be careful. If I find out you didn't use the equilibriator this time—"

The door chime sounded. Carmichael lifted an eyebrow and swiveled in his chair.

"Who is it, Clyde?"

"He gives his name as Robinson, sir. Of Marhew Robotics, he said. He has a bulky package to deliver."

"It must be that new robocook, Father!" Myra Carmichael exclaimed.

"I guess it is. Show him in, Clyde."

Robinson turned out to be a red-faced, efficient-looking little man in greasy overalls and a plaid pullovercoat, who looked disapprovingly at the robutler and strode into the Carmichael living room.

He was followed by a lumbering object about seven feet high, mounted on a pair of rolltreads and swathed completely in quilted rags.

"Got him all wrapped up against the cold, Mr. Carmichael. Lot of delicate circuitry in that job. You ought to be proud of him."

"Clyde, help Mr. Robinson unpack the new robocook," Carmichael said.

"That's okay—I can manage it. And it's *not* a robo-cook, by the way. It's called a roboservitor now. Fancy price, fancy name."

Carmichael heard his wife mutter, "Sam, how much—"

He scowled at her. "Very reasonable, Ethel. Don't worry so much."

He stepped back to admire the roboservitor as it emerged from the quilted swaddling. It was big, all right, with a massive barrel of a chest—robotic controls are always housed in the chest, not in the relatively tiny head —and a gleaming mirror-keen finish that accented its sleekness and newness. Carmichael felt the satisfying glow of pride in ownership. Somehow it seemed to him that he had done something noble and lordly in buying this magnificent robot.

Robinson finished the unpacking job and, standing on tiptoes, opened the robot's chest panel. He unclipped a thick instruction manual and handed it to Carmichael, who stared at the tome uneasily.

"Don't fret about that, Mr. Carmichael. This robot's no trouble to handle. The book's just part of the trimming. Come here a minute."

Carmichael peered into the robot's innards. Pointing, Robinson said. "Here's the recipe bank—biggest and best ever designed. Of course, it's possible to tape in any of your favorite family recipes, if they're not already there. Just hook up your old robocook in the integrator circuit and feed 'em in. I'll take care of that before I leave."

"And what about the—ah—special features?"

"The reducing monitors, you mean? Right over here. See? You just tape in the names of the members of the family and their present and desired weights, and the roboservitor takes care of the rest. Computes caloric in-take, adjusts menus, and everything else."

Carmichael grinned at his wife. "Told you I was going to do something about our weight, Ethel. No more dieting for you, Myra—the robot does all the work." Catching a sour look on his son's face, he added, "And you're not so lean yourself, buster."

"I don't think there'll be any trouble," Robinson said buoyantly. "But if there is, just buzz for me. I handle serv-ice and delivery for Marhew stores in this area."

"Right."

"Now if you'll get me your obsolete robocook, I'll transfer the family recipes before I cart it away on the trade-in deal."

There was a momentary tingle of nostalgia and regret when Robinson left, half an hour later, taking old Jemima with him. Carmichael had almost come to think of the battered '43 Madison as a member of the family. After all, he had bought her sixteen years before, only a couple of years after his marriage.

But she—*it*, he corrected in annoyance—was only a robot, and robots became obsolete. Besides, Jemima prob-ably suffered all the aches and pains of a robot's old age and would be happier dismantled. Carmichael blotted Jemima from his mind.

The four of them spent most of the rest of that evening discovering things about their new roboservitor. Car-michael drew up a table of their weights (himself, 192; Ethel, 145; Myra, 139; Joey, 189) and the amount they proposed to weigh in three months' time (himself, 180; Ethel, 125; Myra, 120; Joey, 175). Carmichael than let his son, who prided himself on his knowledge of practical robotics, integrate the figures and feed them to the robot's programming bank.

"You wish this schedule to take effect immediately?" the roboservitor queried in a deep, mellow bass.

Startled, Carmichael said, "T—tomorrow morning, at breakfast. We might as well start right away."

"He speaks well, doesn't he?" Ethel said.

"He sure does," Joey said. "Jemima always stammered and squeaked, and all she could say was, 'Dinner is served' and 'Be careful, sirr, the soup plate is verry warrm.' "

Carmichael smiled. He noticed his daughter admiring the robot's bulky frame and sleek bronze limbs, and thought resignedly that a seventeen-year-old girl could find the strangest sorts of love objects. But he was happy to see that they were all evidently pleased with the robot. Even with the discount and the trade-in, it *had* been a little on the costly side.

But it would be worth it.

Carmichael slept soundly and woke early, anticipating the first breakfast under the new regime. He still felt pleased with himself.

Dieting had always been such a nuisance, he thought— but, on the other hand, he had never enjoyed the sensation of an annoying roll of fat pushing outward against his elastobelt. He exercised sporadically, but it did little good, and he never had the initiative to keep a rigorous dieting campaign going for long. Now, though, with the mathematics of reducing done effortlessly for him, all the calculating and cooking being handled by the new robot— now, for the first time since he had been Joey's age, he could look forward to being slim and trim once again.

He dressed, showered, and hastily depilated. It was 0730. Breakfast was ready.

Ethel and the children were already at the table when he arrived. Ethel and Myra were munching toast; Joey was peering at a bowl of milkless dry cereal, next to which stood a full glass of milk. Carmichael sat down.

"Your toast, sir," the roboservitor murmured.

Carmichael stared at the single slice. It had already been buttered for him, and the butter had evidently been measured out with a micrometer. The robot proceeded to hand him a cup of black coffee.

He groped for the cream and sugar. They weren't anywhere on the table. The other members of his family were regarding him strangely, and they were curiously, suspiciously silent.

"I like cream and sugar in my coffee," he said to the hovering roboservitor. "Didn't you find that in Jemima's old recipe bank?"

"Of course, sir. But you must learn to drink your coffee without such things, if you wish to lose weight."

Carmichael chuckled. Somehow he had not expected the regimen to be quite like this—quite so, well, Spartan. "Oh, yes. Of course. Ah—are the eggs ready yet?" He considered a day incomplete unless it began with soft-boiled eggs.

"Sorry, no, sir. On Mondays, Wednesdays, and Fridays, breakfast is to consist of toast and black coffee only, except for Master Joey, who gets cereal, fruit juice, and milk."

"I—see."

Well, he had asked for it. He shrugged and took a bite of the toast. He sipped the coffee; it tasted like river mud, but he tried not to make a face.

Joey seemed to be going about the business of eating his cereal rather oddly, Carmichael noticed next. "Why don't you pour that glass of milk *into* the cereal?" he asked. "Won't it taste better that way?"

"Sure it will. But Bismarck says I won't get another glass if I do, so I'm eating it this way."

"Bismarck?"

Joey grinned. "It's the name of a famous nineteenth-century German dictator. They called him the Iron Chancellor." He jerked his head toward the kitchen, to which the roboservitor had silently retreated. "Pretty good name for him, eh?"

"No," said Carmichael. "It's silly."

"It has a certain ring of truth, though," Ethel remarked.

Carmichael did not reply. He finished his toast and coffee somewhat glumly and signaled Clyde to get the car out of the garage. He felt depressed—dieting didn't seem to be so effortless after all, even with the new robot.

As he walked toward the door, the robot glided around him and handed him a small printed slip of paper. Carmichael stared at it. It said:

FRUIT JUICE
LETTUCE & TOMATO SALAD
(ONE) HARD-BOILED EGG
BLACK COFFEE

"What's this thing?"

"You are the only member of this family group who will not be eating three meals a day under my personal supervision. This is your luncheon menu. Please adhere to it," the robot said smoothly.

Repressing a sputter, Carmichael said, "Yes—yes. Of course."

He pocketed the menu and made his way uncertainly to the waiting car.

He was faithful to the robot's orders at lunchtime that

day; even though he was beginning to develop resistance to the idea that had seemed so appealing only the night before, he was willing, at least, to give it a try.

But something prompted him to stay away from the restaurant where Normandy Trust employees usually lunched, and where there were human waiters to smirk at him and fellow executives to ask prying questions.

He ate instead at a cheap robocafeteria two blocks to the north. He slipped in surreptitiously with his collar turned up, punched out his order (it cost him less than a credit altogether), and wolfed it down. He still felt hungry when he was finished, but he compelled himself to return loyally to the office.

He wondered how long he was going to be able to keep up this iron self-control. Not very long, he realized dolefully. And if anyone from the company caught him eating at a robocafeteria, he'd be a laughing stock. Someone of the executive status just *didn't* eat lunch by himself in mechanized cafeterias.

By the time he had finished his day's work, his stomach felt knotted and pleated. His hand was shaky as he punched out his destination on the car's autopanel, and he was thankful that it took less than an hour to get home from the office. Soon, he thought, he'd be tasting food again. Soon. Soon. He switched on the roof-mounted video, leaned back at the recliner, and tried to relax as the car bore him homeward.

He was in for a surprise, though, when he stepped through the safety field into his home. Clyde was waiting as always, and, as always, took his hat and cloak. And, as always, Carmichael reached out for the cocktail that Clyde prepared nightly to welcome him home.

There was no cocktail.

"Are we out of gin, Clyde?"

"No, sir."

"How come no drink, then?"

The robot's rubberized metallic features seemed to droop. "Because, sir, a martini's caloric content is inordinately high. Gin is rated at a hundred calories per ounce and—"

"Oh, no. You, too!"

"Pardon, sir. The new roboservitor has altered my responsive circuits to comply with the regulations now in force in this household."

Carmichael felt his fingers starting to tremble. "Clyde, you've been my butler for almost twenty years."

"Yes, sir."

"You always make my drinks for me. You mix the best martinis in the Western Hemisphere."

"Thank you, sir."

"And you're going to mix one for me right now! That's a direct order!"

"Sir, I—" The robutler staggered wildly and nearly careened into Carmichael. It seemed to have lost all control over its gyro-balance; it clutched agonizedly at its chest panel and started to sag.

Hastily, Carmichael barked, "Order countermanded! Clyde, are you all right?"

Slowly, and with a creak, the robot straightened up. It looked dangerously close to an overload. "Your direct order set up a first-level conflict in me, sir," Clyde whispered faintly. "I—came close to burning out just then, sir. May—may I be excused?"

"Of course. Sorry, Clyde." Carmichael balled his fists. There was such a thing as going too far! The roboservitor —Bismarck—had obviously placed on Clyde a flat prohibition against serving liquor to him. Reducing or no reducing, there were *limits.*

Carmichael strode angrily toward the kitchen.

His wife met him halfway. "I didn't hear you come in, Sam. I want to talk to you about—"

"Later. Where's that robot?"

"In the kitchen, I imagine. It's almost dinnertime."

He brushed past her and swept on into the kitchen, where Bismarck was moving efficiently from electrostove to magnetic worktable. The robot swiveled as Carmichael entered.

"Did you have a good day, sir?"

"No! I'm hungry!"

"The first days of a diet are always the most difficult, Mr. Carmichael. But your body will adjust to the reduction in food intake before long."

"I'm sure of that. But what's this business of tinkering with Clyde?"

"The butler insisted on preparing an alcoholic drink for you. I was forced to adjust his programming. From now on, sir, you may indulge in cocktails on Tuesdays, Thursdays, and Saturdays. I beg to be excused from further discussion, now, sir. The meal is almost ready."

Poor Clyde! Carmichael thought. *And poor me!* He gnashed his teeth impotently a few times, then gave up, and turned away from the glistening, overbearing roboservitor. A light gleamed on the side of the robot's head, indicating that he had shut off the audio circuits and was totally engaged in his task.

Dinner consisted of steak and peas, followed by black coffee. The steak was rare; Carmichael preferred it well done. But Bismarck—the name was beginning to take hold—had had all the latest dietetic theories taped into him, and rare meat it was.

After the robot had cleared the table and tidied up the kitchen, it retired to its storage place in the basement, which gave the Carmichael family a chance to speak openly to each other for the first time that evening.

"Lord!" Ethel snorted. "Sam, I don't object to losing weight, but if we're going to be *tyrannized* in our own home—"

"Mom's right," Joey put in. "It doesn't seem fair for that thing to feed us whatever it pleases. And I didn't like the way it messed around with Clyde's circuits."

Carmichael spread his hands. "I'm not happy about it, either. But we have to give it a try. We can always make readjustments in the programming if it turns out to be necessary."

"But how long are we going to keep this up?" Myra wanted to know. "I had three meals in this house today and I'm starved!"

"Me, too," Joey said. He elbowed himself from his chair and looked around. "Bismarck's downstairs. I'm going to get a slice of lemon pie while the coast is clear."

"No!" Carmichael thundered.

"No?"

"There's no sense in my spending three thousand credits on a dietary robot if you're going to cheat, Joey. I forbid you to have any pie."

"But, Dad, I'm hungry! I'm a growing boy! I'm—"

"You're sixteen years old, and if you grow much more, you won't fit inside the house," Carmichael snapped, looking up at his six-foot-one son.

"Sam, we can't starve the boy," Ethel protested. "If he

wants pie, let him have some. You're carrying this reducing fetish too far."

Carmichael considered that. Perhaps, he thought, I *am*
being a little oversevere. And the thought of lemon pie
was a tempting one. He was pretty hungry himself.

"All right," he said with feigned reluctance. "I guess a
bit of pie won't wreck the plan. In fact, I suppose I'll have
some myself. Joey, why don't you—"

"Begging your pardon," a purring voice said behind
him. Carmichael jumped half an inch. It was the robot,
Bismarck. "It would be most unfortunate if you were to
have pie now, Mr. Carmichael. My calculations are very
precise."

Carmichael saw the angry gleam in his son's eye, but
the robot seemed extraordinarily big at that moment, and
it happened to stand between him and the kitchen.

He sighed weakly. "Let's forget the lemon pie, Joey."

After two full days of the Bismarckian diet, Carmichael
discovered that his inner resources of will power were
beginning to crumble. On the third day he tossed away
the printed lunchtime diet and went out irresponsibly with
MacDougal and Hennessey for a six-course lunch, complete with cocktails. It seemed to him that he hadn't tasted
real food since the robot arrived.

That night, he was able to tolerate the seven-hundred-
calorie dinner without any inward grumblings, being still
well lined with lunch. But Ethel and Myra and Joey were
increasingly irritable. It seemed that the robot had usurped
Ethel's job of handling the daily marketing and had
stocked in nothing but a huge supply of low-calorie foods.
The larder now bulged with wheat germ, protein bread,
irrigated salmon, and other hitherto unfamiliar items.
Myra had taken up biting her nails; Joey's mood was one

of black, sullen brooding, and Carmichael knew how that could lead to trouble quickly with a sixteen-year-old.

After the meager dinner, he ordered Bismarck to go to the basement and stay there until summoned.

The robot said, "I advise you, sir, that I will detect indulgence in any forbidden foods in my absence and adjust for it in the next meals."

"You have my word," Carmichael said, thinking it was indeed queer to have to pledge on your honor to your own robot. He waited until the massive servitor had vanished below; then he turned to Joey and said, "Get the instruction manual, boy."

Joey grinned in understanding. Ethel said, "Sam, what are you going to do?"

Carmichael patted his shrunken waistline. "I'm going to take a can opener to that creature and adjust his programming. He's overdoing this diet business. Joey, have you found the instructions on how to reprogram the robot?"

"Page one hundred and sixty-seven. I'll get the tool kit, Dad."

"Right." Carmichael turned to the robutler, who was standing by dumbly, in his usual forward-stooping posture of expectancy. "Clyde, go down below and tell Bismarck we want him right away."

Moments later, the two robots appeared. Carmichael said to the roboservitor, "I'm afraid it's necessary for us to change your program. We've overestimated our capacity for losing weight."

"I beg you to reconsider, sir. Extra weight is harmful to every vital organ in the body. I plead with you to maintain my scheduling unaltered."

"I'd rather cut my own throat. Joey, inactivate him and do your stuff."

Grinning fiercely, the boy stepped forward and pressed the stud that opened the robot's ribcage. A frightening assortment of gears, cams, and translucent cables became visible inside the robot. With a small wrench in one hand and the open instruction book in the other, Joey prepared to make the necessary changes, while Carmichael held his breath and a pall of silence descended on the living room. Even old Clyde leaned forward to have a better view.

Joey muttered, "Lever F two, with the yellow indicia, is to be advanced one notch . . . umm. Now twist dial B nine to the left, thereby opening the taping compartment and—oops!"

Carmichael heard the clang of a wrench and saw the bright flare of sparks; Joey leaped back, cursing with surprisingly mature skill. Ethel and Myra gasped simultaneously.

"What happened?" four voices—Clyde's coming in last—demanded.

"Dropped the damn wrench," Joey said. "I guess I shorted out something in there."

The robot's eyes were whirling satanically and its voice box was emitting an awesome twelve-cycle rumble. The great metal creature stood stiffly in the middle of the living room; with brusque gestures of its big hands, it slammed shut the open chest plates.

"We'd better call Mr. Robinson," Ethel said worriedly. "A short-circuited robot is likely to explode, or worse."

"We should have called Robinson in the first place," Carmichael murmured bitterly. "It's my fault for letting Joey tinker with an expensive and delicate mechanism like that. Myra, get me the card Mr. Robinson left."

"Gee, Dad, this is the first time I've ever had anything like that go wrong," Joey insisted. "I didn't know——".

"You're darned right you didn't know." Carmichael took the card from his daughter and started toward the phone. "I hope we can reach him at this hour. If we can't——"

Suddenly Carmichael felt cold fingers prying the card from his hand. He was so startled he relinquished it without a struggle. He watched as Bismarck efficiently ripped it into little fragments and shoved them into a wall disposal unit.

The robot said, "There will be no further meddling with my program tapes." Its voice was deep and strangely harsh.

"What——"

"Mr. Carmichael, today you violated the program I set down for you. My perceptors reveal that you consumed an amount far in excess of your daily lunchtime requirement."

"Sam, what——"

"Quiet, Ethel. Bismarck, I order you to shut yourself off at once."

"My apologies, sir. I cannot serve you if I am shut off."

"I don't *want* you to serve me. You're out of order. I want you to remain still until I can phone the repairman and get him to service you."

Then he remembered the card that had gone into the disposal unit. He felt a faint tremor of apprehension.

"You took Robinson's card and destroyed it."

"Further alteration of my circuits would be detrimental to the Carmichael family," said the robot. "I cannot permit you to summon the repairman."

"Don't get him angry, Dad," Joey warned. "I'll call the police. I'll be back in——"

"You will remain within this house," the robot said. Moving with impressive speed on its oiled treads, it crossed the room, blocking the door, and reached far above its head to activate the impassable privacy field that protected the house. Carmichael watched, aghast, as the inexorable robotic fingers twisted and manipulated the field controls.

"I have now reversed the polarity of the house privacy field," the robot announced. "Since you are obviously not to be trusted to keep to the diet I prescribe, I cannot allow you to leave the premises. You will remain within and continue to obey my beneficial advice."

Calmly, he uprooted the telephone. Next, the windows were opaqued and the stud broken off. Finally, the robot seized the instruction book from Joey's numbed hands and shoved it into the disposal unit.

"Breakfast will be served at the usual time," Bismarck said mildly. "For optimum purposes of health, you are all to be asleep by 2300 hours. I shall leave you now, until morning. Good night."

Carmichael did not sleep well that night, nor did he eat well the next day. He awoke late, for one thing—well past nine. He discovered that someone, obviously Bismarck, had neatly canceled out the impulses from the housebrain that woke him at seven each morning.

The breakfast menu was toast and black coffee. Carmichael ate disgruntedly, not speaking, indicating by brusque scowls that he did not want to be spoken to. After the miserable meal had been cleared away, he surreptitiously tiptoed to the front door in his dressing gown and darted a hand toward the handle.

The door refused to budge. He pushed until sweat dribbled down his face. He heard Ethel whisper warningly, "*Sam*—" and a moment later cool metallic fingers gently disengaged him from the door.

Bismarck said, "I beg your pardon, sir. The door will not open. I explained this last night."

Carmichael gazed sourly at the gimmicked control box of the privacy field. The robot had them utterly hemmed in. The reversed privacy field made it impossible for them to leave the house; it cast a sphere of force around the entire detached dwelling. In theory, the field could be penetrated from outside, but nobody was likely to come calling without an invitation. Not here in Westley. It wasn't one of those neighborly subdivisions where everybody knew everybody else. Carmichael had picked it for that reason.

"Damn you," he growled, "you can't hold us *prisoners* in here!"

"My intent is only to help you," said the robot, in a mechanical yet dedicated voice. "My function is to supervise your diet. Since you will not obey willingly, obedience must be enforced—for your own good."

Carmichael scowled and walked away. The worst part of it was that the roboservitor sounded so *sincere!*

Trapped. The phone connection was severed. The windows were darkened. Somehow, Joey's attempt at repairs had resulted in a short-circuit of the robot's obedience filters, and had also exaggeratedly stimulated its sense of function. Now Bismarck was determined to make them lose weight if it had to kill them to do so.

And that seemed very likely.

Blockaded, the Carmichael family met in a huddled little group to whisper plans for a counterattack. Clyde stood watch, but the robutler seemed to be in a state of general shock since the demonstration of the servitor-robot's independent capacity for action, and Carmichael now regarded him as undependable.

"He's got the kitchen walled off with some kind of

electronic-based force web," Joey said. "He must have built it during the night. I tried to sneak in and scrounge some food, and got nothing but a flat nose for trying."

"I know," Carmichael said sadly. "He built the same sort of doohickey around the bar. Three hundred credits of good booze in there and I can't even grab the handle!"

"This is no time to worry about drinking," Ethel said morosely. "We'll be skeletons any day."

"It isn't *that* bad, Mom!" Joey said.

"Yes, it is!" cried Myra. "I've lost five pounds in four days!"

"Is that so terrible?"

"I'm wasting away," she sobbed. "My figure—it's vanishing! And—"

"Quiet," Carmichael whispered. "Bismarck's coming!"

The robot emerged from the kitchen, passing through the force barrier as if it had been a cobweb. It seemed to have effect on humans only, Carmichael thought. "Lunch will be served in eight minutes," it said obsequiously, and returned to its lair.

Carmichael glanced at his watch. The time was 1230 hours. "Probably down at the office they're wondering where I am," he said. "I haven't missed a day's work in years."

"They won't care," Ethel said. "An executive isn't required to account for every day off he takes, you know."

"But they'll worry after three or four days, won't they?" Myra asked. "Maybe they'll try to phone—or even send a rescue mission!"

From the kitchen, Bismarck said coldly, "There will be no danger of that. While you slept this morning, I notified your place of employment that you were resigning."

Carmichael gasped. Then, recovering, he said: "You're

lying! The phone's cut off—and you never would have risked leaving the house, even if we *were* asleep!"

"I communicated with them via a microwave generator I constructed with the aid of your son's reference books last night," Bismarck replied. "Clyde reluctantly supplied me with the number. I also phoned your bank and instructed them to handle for you all such matters as tax payments, investment decisions, etc. To forestall difficulties, let me add that a force web will prevent access on your part to the electronic equipment in the basement. I will be able to conduct such communication with the outside world as will be necessary for your welfare, Mr. Carmichael. You need have no worries on that score."

"No," Carmichael echoed hollowly. "No worries."

He turned to Joey. "We've got to get out of here. Are you sure there's no way of disconnecting the privacy field?"

"He's got one of his force fields rigged around the control box. I can't even get near the thing."

"If only we had an iceman, or an oilman, the way the oldtime houses did," Ethel said bitterly. "He'd show up and come inside and probably he'd know how to shut the field off. But not *here*. Oh, no. We've got a shiny chrome-plated cryostat in the basement that dishes out lots of liquid helium to run the fancy cryotronic supercooled power plant that gives us heat and light, and we have enough food in the freezer to last for at least a decade or two, and so we can live like this for years, a neat little self-contained island in the middle of civilization, with nobody bothering us, nobody wondering about us, and Sam Carmichael's pet robot to feed us whenever and as little as it pleases—"

There was a cutting edge to her voice that was dangerously close to hysteria.

"Ethel, please," said Carmichael.

"Please what? Please keep quiet? Please stay calm? Sam, we're *prisoners* in here!"

"I know. You don't have to raise your voice."

"Maybe if I do, someone will hear us and come get us out," she replied more coolly.

"It's four hundred feet to the next home, dear. And in the seven years we've lived here, we've had about two visits from our neighbors. We paid a stiff price for seclusion and now we're paying a stiffer one. But please keep under control, Ethel."

"Don't worry, Mom. I'll figure a way out of this," Joey said reassuringly.

In one corner of the living room, Myra was sobbing quietly to herself, blotching her make-up. Carmichael felt a faintly claustrophobic quiver. The house was big, three levels and twelve rooms, but even so he could get tired of it very quickly.

"Luncheon is served," the roboservitor announced in booming tones.

And tired of lettuce-and-tomato lunches, too, Carmichael added silently, as he shepherded his family toward the dining room for their meager midday meal.

"You have to do *something* about this, Sam," Ethel Carmichael said on the third day of their imprisonment.

He glared at her. "Have to, eh? And just what am I supposed to do?"

"Daddy, don't get excited," Myra said.

He whirled on her. "Don't tell me what I should or shouldn't do!"

"She can't help it, dear. We're all a little overwrought. After all, cooped up here—"

"I know. Like lambs in a pen," he finished acidly. "Except that we're not being fattened for slaughter. We're—we're being *thinned*, and for our own alleged good!"

Carmichael subsided gloomily. Toast-and-black-coffee, lettuce-and-tomato, rare-steak-and-peas. Bismarck's channels seemed to have frozen permanently at that daily menu.

But what could he do?

Contact with the outside world was impossible. The robot had erected a bastion in the basement from which he conducted such little business with the world as the Carmichael family had. Generally, they were self-sufficient. And Bismarck's force fields insured the impossibility of any attempts to disconnect the outer sheath, break into the basement, or even get at the food supply or the liquor. It was all very neat, and all four of them were fast approaching a state of starvation.

"Sam?"

He lifted his head wearily. "What is it, Ethel?"

"Myra had an idea before. Tell him, Myra."

"Oh, it would never work," Myra said demurely.

"Tell *him!*"

"Well—Dad, you could try to turn Bismarck off."

"Huh?" Carmichael grunted.

"I mean if you or Joey could distract him somehow, then Joey or you could open him up again and—"

"No," Carmichael snapped. "That thing's seven feet tall and weighs three hundred pounds. If you think *I'm* going to wrestle with it—"

"We could let Clyde try," Ethel suggested.

Carmichael shook his head vehemently. "The carnage would be frightful."

Joey said, "Dad, it may be our only hope."

"You too?" Carmichael asked.

He took a deep breath. He felt himself speared by two deadly feminine glances, and he knew there was no hope but to try it. Resignedly, he pushed himself to his feet and said, "Okay. Clyde, go call Bismarck. Joey, I'll try to hang onto his arms while you open up his chest. Yank anything you can."

"Be careful," Ethel warned. "If there's an explosion—"

"If there's an explosion, we're all free," Carmichael said testily. He turned to see the broad figure of the roboservitor standing at the entrance to the living room.

"May I be of service, sir?"

"You may," Carmichael said. "We're having a little debate here and we want your evidence. It's a matter of defannising the poozlestan and—*Joey, open him up!*"

Carmichael grabbed for the robot's arms, trying to hold them without getting hurled across the room, while his son clawed frantically at the stud that opened the robot's innards. Carmichael anticipated immediate destruction— but, to his surprise, he found himself slipping as he tried to grasp the thick arms.

"Dad, it's no use. I—he—"

Carmichael found himself abruptly four feet off the ground. He heard Ethel and Myra scream and Clyde's, "*Do* be careful, sir."

Bismarck was carrying them across the room, gently, cradling him in one giant arm and Joey in the other. It set them down on the couch and stood back.

"Such an attempt is highly dangerous," Bismarck said reprovingly. "It puts me in danger of harming you physically. Please avoid any such acts in the future."

Carmichael stared broodingly at his son. "Did you have the same trouble I did?"

Joey nodded. "I couldn't get within an inch of his skin.

It stands to reason, though. He's built one of those damned force screens around *himself*, too."

Carmichael groaned. He did not look at his wife and his children. Physical attack of Bismarck was now out of the question. He began to feel as if he had been condemned to life imprisonment—and that his stay in durance would not be extremely prolonged.

In the upstairs bathroom, six days after the beginning of the blockade, Sam Carmichael stared at his haggard fleshless face in the mirror before wearily climbing on the scale.

He weighed 180.

He had lost twelve pounds in less than two weeks. He was fast becoming a quivering wreck.

A thought occurred to him as he stared at the wavering needle on the scale, and sudden elation spread over him. He dashed downstairs. Ethel was doggedly crocheting in the living room; Joey and Myra were playing cards grimly, desperately now, after six solid days of gin rummy and honeymoon bridge.

"Where's that robot?" Carmichael roared. "Come out here!"

"In the kitchen," Ethel said tonelessly.

"Bismarck! Bismarck!" Carmichael roared. "Come out here!"

The robot appeared. "How may I serve you, sir?"

"Damn you, scan me with your superpower receptors and tell me how much I weigh!"

After a pause, the robot said gravely, "One hundred seventy-nine pounds eleven ounces, Mr. Carmichael."

"Yes! Yes! And the original program I had taped into you was supposed to reduce me from 192 to 180," Carmichael crowed triumphantly. "So I'm finished with you, as long as I don't gain any more weight. And so are the rest of us, I'll bet. Ethel! Myra! Joey! Upstairs and weigh yourselves!"

But the robot regarded him with a doleful glare and said, "Sir, I find no record within me of any limitation on your reduction of weight."

"*What*?"

"I have checked my tapes fully. I have a record of an order causing weight reduction, but that tape does not appear to specify a *terminus ad quem*."

Carmichael exhaled and took three staggering steps backward. His legs wobbled; he felt Joey supporting him. He mumbled, "But I thought—I'm sure we did—I *know* we instructed you—"

Hunger gnawed at his flesh. Joey said softly, "Dad, probably that part of his tape was erased when he short-circuited."

"Oh," Carmichael said numbly.

He tottered into the living room and collapsed heavily in what had once been his favorite armchair. It wasn't any more. The entire house had become odious to him. He longed to see the sunlight again, to see trees and grass, even to see that excrescence of an ultramodern house that the left-hand neighbors had erected.

But now that would be impossible. He had hoped, for a few minutes at least, that the robot would release them from dietary bondage when the original goal was shown to be accomplished. Evidently that was to be denied him. He giggled, then began to laugh.

"What's so funny, dear?" Ethel asked. She had lost her earlier tendency to hysteria, and after long days of complex crocheting now regarded the universe with quiet resignation.

"Funny? The fact that I weigh one eighty now. I'm lean, trim, fit as a fiddle. Next month I'll weigh one seventy. Then one sixty. Then finally about eighty-eight pounds or so. We'll all shrivel up. Bismarck will starve us to death."

"Don't worry, Dad. We're going to get out of this."

Somehow Joey's brash boyish confidence sounded forced now. Carmichael shook his head. "We won't. We'll never get out. And Bismarck's going to reduce us *ad infinitum*. He's got no *terminus ad quem*!"

"What's he saying?" Myra asked.

"It's Latin," Joey explained. "But listen, Dad—I have an idea that I think will work." He lowered his voice. "I'm going to try to adjust Clyde, see? If I can get a sort of multiphase vibrating effect in his neural pathway, maybe I can slip him through the privacy field. He can go get help, find someone who can shut the field off. There's an article on multiphase generators in last month's *Popular Electromagnetics* and it's in my room upstairs. I—"

His voice died away. Carmichael, who had been listening with the air of a condemned man hearing his reprieve, said impatiently, "Well? Go on. Tell me more."

"Didn't you hear that, Dad?"

"Hear what?"

"The front door. I thought I heard it open just now."

"We're all cracking up," Carmichael said dully. He cursed the salesman at Marhew, he cursed the inventor of cryotonic robots, he cursed the day he had first felt ashamed of good old Jemima and resolved to replace her with a new model.

"I hope I'm not intruding, Mr. Carmichael," a new voice said apologetically.

Carmichael blinked and looked up. A wiry, ruddy-cheeked figure in a heavy peajacket had materialized in the middle of the living room. He was clutching a green metal toolbox in one gloved hand. He was Robinson, the robot repairman.

Carmichael said hoarsely, "How did *you* get in?"

"Through the front door. I could see a light on inside, but nobody answered the doorbell when I rang, so I stepped in. Your doorbell's out of order. I thought I'd tell you. I know it's rude—"

"Don't apologize," Carmichael muttered. "We're delighted to see you."

"I was in the neighborhood, you see, and I figured I'd drop in and see how things were working out with your new robot," Robinson said.

Carmichael told him crisply and precisely and quickly. "So we've been prisoners in here for six days," he finished. "And your robot is gradually starving us to death. We can't hold out much longer."

The smile abruptly left Robinson's cheery face. "I *thought* you all looked rather unhealthy. Oh, damn, now there'll be an investigation and all kinds of trouble. But at least I can end your imprisonment."

He opened his toolbox and selected a tubular instrument eight inches long, with a glass bulb at one end and a trigger attachment at the other. "Force-field damper," he explained. He pointed it at the control box of the privacy field and nodded in satisfaction. "There. Great little gadget. That neutralizes the effects of what the robot did and you're no longer blockaded. And now, if you'll produce the robot—"

Carmichael sent Clyde off to get Bismarck. The robutler returned a few moments later, followed by the looming roboservitor. Robinson grinned gaily, pointed the neutralizer at Bismarck and squeezed. The robot froze in midglide, emitting a brief squeak.

"There. That should immobilize him. Let's have a look in that chassis now."

The repairman quickly opened Bismarck's chest and, producing a pocket flash, peered around in the complex interior of the servomechanism, making occasional clucking inaudible comments.

Overwhelmed with relief, Carmichael shakily made his way to a seat. Free! Free at last. His mouth watered at the thought of the meals he was going to have in the next few days. Potatoes and martinis and warm buttered rolls and all the other forbidden foods!

"Fascinating," Robinson said, half to himself. "The obedience filters are completely shorted out, and the purpose nodes were somehow soldered together by the momentary high-voltage arc. I've never seen anything quite like this, you know."

"Neither had we," Carmichael said hollowly.

"Really, though—this is an utterly new breakthrough in robotic science! If we can reproduce this effect, it means we can build self-willed robots—and think of what *that* means to science!"

"We know already," Ethel said.

"I'd love to watch what happens when the power source is operating," Robinson went on. "For instance, is that feedback loop really negative or—"

"No!" five voices shrieked at once—with Clyde, as usual, coming in late.

It was too late. The entire event had taken no more than a tenth of a second. Robinson had squeezed his neutralizer trigger again, activating Bismarck—and in one quick swoop the roboservitor seized the neutralizer and toolbox from the stunned repairman, activated the privacy field once again, and exultantly crushed the fragile neutralizer between two mighty fingers.

Robinson stammered, "But—but—"

"This attempt at interfering with the well-being of the Carmichael family was ill-advised," Bismarck said severely. He peered into the toolbox, found a second neutralizer, and neatly reduced it to junk. He clanged shut his chest plates.

Robinson turned and streaked for the door, forgetting the reactivated privacy field. He bounced back hard, spinning wildly around. Carmichael rose from his seat just in time to catch him.

There was a panicky, trapped look on the repairman's face. Carmichael was no longer able to share the emotion; inwardly he was numb, totally resigned, not minded for further struggle.

"He—he moved so *fast!*" Robinson burst out.

"He did indeed," Carmichael said tranquilly. He patted his hollow stomach and sighed gently. "Luckily, we have an unoccupied guest bedroom for you, Mr. Robinson. Welcome to our happy little home. I hope you like toast and black coffee for breakfast."

Mugwump Four

·····➤◉◄····

AL MILLER was only trying to phone the Friendly Finance Corporation to ask about an extension on his loan. It was a Murray Hill number, and he had dialed as far as MU-4 when the receiver clicked queerly and a voice said, "Come in, Operator Nine. Operator Nine, do you read me?"

Al frowned. "I don't want the operator. There must be something wrong with my phone if—"

"Just a minute. Who *are* you?"

"I ought to ask *you* that," Al said. "What are you doing on the other end, anyway? I hadn't even finished dialing. I got as far as MU four and—"

"Well? You dialed MUgwump four and you got us. What more do you want?" A suspicious pause. "Say, you aren't Operator Nine!"

"No, I'm *not* Operator Nine, and I'm trying to dial a Murray Hill number, and how about getting off the line?"

"Hold it, friend. Are you a Normal?"

Al blinked. "Yeah—yeah, I like to think so."

"So how'd you know the number?"

"Dammit, I *didn't* know the number! I was trying to call someone, and all of a sudden the phone cut out and I got you, whoever the blazes *you* are."

"I'm the communications warden at MUgwump four," the other said crisply. "And you're a suspicious individual. We'll have to investigate you."

The telephone emitted a sudden burping sound. Al felt as if his feet had grown roots. He could not move at all. It was awkward to be standing there at his own telephone in the privacy of his own room, as unbending as a steel girder. Time still moved, he saw. The hand on the big clock above the phone had just shifted from 3:30 to 3:31.

Sweat rivered down his back as he struggled to put down the phone. He fought to lift his left foot. He strained to twitch his right eyelid. No go on all counts; he was frozen, all but his chest muscles—thank goodness for that.

Several minutes later, matters became even more awkward when his front door, which had been locked, opened abruptly. Three strangers entered. They looked oddly alike: a trio of Tweedledums, no more than five feet high, wide through the waist, jowly of face and balding of head, each wearing an inadequate single-breasted blue serge suit.

Al discovered he could roll his eyes. He rolled them. He wanted to apologize because his unexpected paralysis kept him from acting the proper part of a host, but his tongue would not obey. And on second thought, it occurred to him that the little bald men might be connected in some way with that paralysis.

The reddest-faced of the three little men hung up the telephone and the stasis ended. Al nearly folded up as the tension that gripped him broke. He said, "Just who the deuce—"

"*We* will ask the questions. You are Al Miller?"

Al nodded.

"And obviously you are a Normal. So there has been a grave error. Mordecai, examine the telephone."

The second little man picked up the phone and calmly disemboweled it with three involved motions of his stubby hands. He frowned over the telephone's innards for a moment; then, humming tunelessly, he produced a wire clipper and severed the telephone cord.

"Hold on here!" Al burst out. "You can't just rip out my phone like that! You aren't from the phone company!"

"Quiet," said the spokesman nastily. "Well, Mordecai?"

The second little man said, "Probability one to one million. The cranch interval overlapped and his telephone matrix slipped. His call was piped into our wire by error, Waldemar."

"So he isn't a spy?" Waldemar asked.

"Doubtful. As you see, he's of rudimentary intelligence. His dialing our number was a statistical fluke."

"But now he knows about us," said the third little man in a surprisingly deep voice. "I vote for demoleculariza-tion."

The other two whirled on their companion. "Always bloodthirsty, eh, Giovanni?" said Mordecai. "You'd vio-late the code at the snap of a meson."

"There won't be any demolecularization while *I'm* in charge," added Waldemar.

"What do we do with him then?" Giovanni demanded.

Mordecai said, "Freeze him and take him down to Headquarters. He's *their* problem."

"I think this has gone about as far as it's going to go," Al exploded at last. "However you three creeps got in here, you'd better get yourselves right out again, or—"

"Enough," Waldemar said.

Al felt his jaws stiffen. He realized bewilderedly that he was frozen again. And frozen, this time, with his mouth gaping foolishly open.

The trip took about five minutes, and so far as Al was concerned, it was one long blur. At the end of the journey, the blur lifted for an instant, long enough to give Al one good glimpse of his surroundings—a residential street in what might have been Brooklyn or Queens (or Cincinnati or Detroit, he thought morbidly)—before he was hustled into the basement of a two-family house. He found himself in a windowless, brightly lit chamber cluttered with complex-looking machinery and with a dozen or so alarmingly identical little baldheaded men. Not until then did his paralysis lift.

The chubbiest of the bunch glared sourly at him and asked, "Are you a spy?"

"I'm just an innocent bystander," Al said earnestly. "I picked up my phone and started to dial, and all of a sudden some guy asked me if I was Operator Nine. Honest, that's all."

"Overlapping of the cranch interval," muttered Mordecai. "Slipped matrix."

"Umm. Unfortunate," the chubby one commented. "We'll have to dispose of him."

"Demolecularization is the best way," Giovanni put in immediately.

"Dispose of him *humanely*, I mean. It's revolting to think of taking the life of an inferior being. But he simply can't remain in this fourspace any longer, not if he knows."

"But I *don't* know!" Al protested. "I couldn't be more mixed up if I tried! Won't you please tell me—"

"Very well," said the pudgiest one, who seemed to be the leader. "Waldemar, tell him about us."

Waldemar said, "You're now in the local headquarters of a secret mutant group working for the overthrow of humanity as you know it. By some accident, you happened to dial our private communication exchange, MUtant four—"

"I thought it was MUgwump four," Al interjected.

"The code name, naturally," said Waldemar. "To continue: you channeled into our communication network. You now know too much. Your presence in this space–time nexus jeopardizes the success of the entire movement. Therefore we are forced—"

"—to demolecularize—" Giovanni began.

"—to dispose of you," Waldemar continued sternly. "We're humane beings—most of us—and we won't do anything that would make you suffer. But you can't stay in this area of space–time, can you?"

Al shook his head dimly. These little potbellied men were mutants working for the overthrow of humanity? Well, he had no reason to think they were lying to him. The world was full of little potbellied men. Maybe they were all part of the secret organization.

"Look," he said, "I didn't *want* to dial your number. It was all a silly accident. But I'm a fair guy. Let me get out of here and I'll keep mum about the whole thing. You can go ahead and overthrow humanity, if that's what you want to do. I promise not to interfere in any way. If you're mutants, you ought to be able to look into my mind and see that I'm sincere—"

"We have no telepathic powers," declared the chubby leader curtly. "If we had, there would be no need for a communications network in the first place. In the second place, your sincerity is not the issue. We have enemies. If you were to fall into their hands—"

"I won't say a word! Even if they torture me—brainwash me—I swear I'll keep quiet!"

"No. At this stage in our campaign, we can take no risks. You'll have to go. Prepare the temporal centrifuge, Mordecai."

Four of the little men, led by Mordecai, unveiled a complicated-looking device of the general size and shape of a concrete mixer. Waldemar and Giovanni shoved Al toward the machine. It came rapidly to life: dials glowed, indicator needles teetered, loud buzzes and clicks implied readiness.

Al said nervously, "What are you going to do to me?"

"This machine will hurl you forward in time," Waldemar explained. "Too bad we have to rip you right out of your temporal matrix, but we've no choice. You'll be well taken care of up ahead, though. No doubt, by the twenty-fifth century, our kind will have taken over completely. You'll be the last of the Normals. Practically a living fossil. You'll love it. You'll be a walking museum piece."

"Assuming the machine works," Giovanni put in maliciously. "We don't really know if it does, you see."

Al gaped. They were busily strapping him to a cold copper slab in the heart of the machine. "You don't even know if it *works*?"

"Not really," Waldemar admitted. "Present theory holds that time-travel works only one way—forward. So we haven't been able to recover any of our test specimens and see how they reacted. Of course, they *do* vanish when the machine is turned on, so we know they must go *somewhere.*"

"Oh," Al said weakly.

He was trussed in thoroughly. Experimental wriggling of his right wrist showed him that. But even if he could get loose, these weird little men would only freeze him and put him into the machine again.

His shoulders slumped resignedly. He wondered if anyone would miss him. The Friendly Finance Corporation certainly would. But since, in a sense, it was their fault he was in this mess now, he couldn't get very upset about that. They could always sue his estate for the $300 he owed them, if his estate was worth that much.

Nobody else was going to mind the disappearance of Albert Miller from the space–time continuum, he thought dourly. His parents were dead, he hadn't seen his one sister in fifteen years, and the girl he used to know in Topeka was married and at last report had three kids.

Still and all, he liked 1959. He wasn't sure how he would take to the twenty-fifth century—or the twenty-fifth century to him.

"Ready for temporal discharge," Mordecai sang out.

The chubby leader peered up at Al. "We're sorry about all this, you understand. But nothing and nobody can be allowed to stand in the way of the Cause."

"Sure," Al said. "I understand."

The concrete-mixer part of the machine began to revolve, bearing Al with it as it built up tempokinetic potential. Momentum increased alarmingly. In the background, Al heard an ominous droning sound that grew louder and louder, until it drowned out everything else. His head reeled. The room and its fat little mutants went blurry. He heard a *pop!* like the sound of a breaking balloon.

It was the rupturing of the space–time continuum. Al Miller went hurtling forward along the fourspace track, head first. He shut his eyes and hoped for the best.

When the dizziness stopped, he found himself sitting in the middle of an impeccably clean, faintly yielding roadway, staring up at the wheels of vehicles swishing by overhead at phenomenal speeds. After a moment or two more, he realized they were not airborne, but simply automobiles racing along an elevated roadway, made of some practically invisible substance.

So the temporal centrifuge *had* worked!

Al glanced around. A crowd was collecting. A couple of hundred people had formed a big circle. They were pointing and muttering. Nobody approached closer than fifty or sixty feet.

They weren't potbellied mutants. Without exception, they were all straight-backed six-footers with full heads of hair. The women were tall, too. Men and women alike were dressed in a sort of tuniclike garment made of iridescent material that constantly changed colors.

A gong began to ring, rapidly peaking in volume. Al scrambled to his feet and put on a tentative smile.

"My name's Miller. I come from 1959. Would somebody mind telling me what year this is, and—"

He was drowned out by two hundred voices screaming in terror. The crowd stampeded away, dashing madly in every direction, as if he were some ferocious monster. The gong continued to clang loudly. Cars hummed overhead.

Al saw a squat, beetle-shaped black vehicle coming toward him on the otherwise empty road. The car pulled up half a block away, the top sprang open, and a figure clad in what might have been a driver's suit—or a spacesuit—stepped out and advanced toward Al.

"Dozzinon murrifar volan," the armored figure called out.

"No speak," Al replied. "I'm a stranger here."

To his dismay, he saw the other draw something shaped like a weapon and point it at him. Al's hands shot immediately into the air. A globe of bluish light exuded from the broad nozzle of the gun, hung suspended for a moment, and drifted toward Al. He dodged uneasily to one side, but the globe of light followed him, descended, and wrapped itself around him.

It was like being on the inside of a soap bubble. He could see out, though distortedly. He touched the curving side of the globe in a cautious way; it was resilient and springy to the touch, but his fingers did not go through.

He noticed with some misgiving that his bubble-cage was starting to drift off the ground. It trailed a ropelike extension, which the man in the armored suit deftly grabbed and knotted to the rear bumper of his car. He drove quickly away—with Al, bobbing in his impenetrable bubble of light, tagging helplessly along like a captured Gaul being dragged through the streets of Rome behind a chariot—but several feet in the air.

He got used to the irregular motion after a while and relaxed enough to be able to study his surroundings. He was passing through a remarkably antiseptic-looking city, free from refuse and dust. Towering buildings, all bright and spankingly new-looking, shot up everywhere. People goggled at him from the safety of the pedestrian walkways as he jounced past.

After about ten minutes, the car halted outside an imposing building whose façade bore the words ISTFAQ BARNOLL. Three men in armored suits appeared from within to flank Al's captor as a kind of honor guard. Al was borne within.

He was nudged gently into a small room on the ground floor. The door rolled shut behind him and seemed to join to the rest of the wall; no division line was apparent. A moment later, the balloon popped open, and just in time, too; the air had been getting quite stale inside it.

Al glanced around. A square window opened in the wall and three grim-faced men peered intently at him from an adjoining cubicle.

A voice from a speaker grid above Al's head said, "Murrifar althrosk?"

"Al Miller, from the twentieth century. And it wasn't my idea to come here, believe me."

"Durberal haznik? Quittimar?"

Al shrugged. "No parley-voo. Honest, I don't savvy."

His three investigators conferred among themselves—taking what seemed to Al the needless precaution of switching off the mike to prevent him from overhearing their deliberations.

He saw one of the men leave the observation cubicle. When the man returned, some five minutes later, he brought with him a tall, gloomy-looking man wearing an impressive spade-shaped beard.

The mike was turned on again. Spadebeard said rumblingly, "How be thou hight?"

"Eh?"

"An thou reck the King's tongue, I conjure thee speak!"

Al grinned. No doubt they had fetched an expert in dead languages to talk to him. "Right language, but the wrong time. I'm from the twentieth century, not the tenth. Come forward a ways."

Spadebeard paused to change mental gears. "A thousand pardons—I mean *sorry*. Wrong idiom. Dig me now?"

"I follow you. What year is this?"

"It is 2431. And from whence be you?"

"You don't quite have it straight yet, but I'm from 1959."

"And how came you hither?"

"I wish I knew," Al said. "I was just trying to phone the loan company, see? Anyway, I got involved with these little fat guys who wanted to take over the world. Mutants, they said they were. And they decided they had to get rid of me, so they bundled me into their time machine and shot me forward. So I'm here."

"A spy of the mutated ones, eh?"

"Spy? Who said anything about a spy? Talk about jumping to conclusions! I'm—"

"You have been sent by them to wreak mischief among us. No transparent story of yours will deceive us. You are not the first to come to our era, you know. And you will meet the same fate the others met."

Al shook his head foggily. "Look here, you're making a big mistake. I'm not a spy for anybody. And I don't want to get involved in any war between you and the mutants—"

"The war is over. The last of the mutated ones was exterminated fifty years ago."

"Okay, then. What can you fear from me? Honest, I don't want to cause any trouble. If the mutants are wiped out, how could my spying help them?"

"No action in time and space is ever absolute. In our fourspace, the mutuants are eradicated—but they lurk elsewhere, waiting for their chance to enter and spread destruction."

Al's brain was swimming. "Let's let that pass. I'm not a spy. I just want to be left alone. Let me settle down here somewhere—put me on probation, show me the ropes, stake me to a few credits, or whatever you use for money here. I won't make any trouble."

"Your body teems with microorganisms of diseases long extinct in this world. Only the fact that we were able to confine you in a force-bubble almost as soon as you arrived here saved us from a terrible epidemic of ancient diseases."

"A couple of injections, that's all, and you can kill any bacteria on or in me," Al pleaded. "You're advanced people. You ought to be able to do a simple thing like that."

"And then there is the matter of your genetic structure," Spadebeard continued inexorably. "You bear genes long since eliminated from humanity as undesirable. Permitting you to remain here, breeding furtively, would introduce unutterable confusion. Perhaps you carry latently the same mutant strain that cost humanity so many centuries of bloodshed!"

"No," Al protested. "Look at me. I'm pretty tall, no potbelly, a full head of hair—"

"The gene is recessive. But it crops up unexpectedly."

"I solemnly promise to control my breeding," Al declared. "I won't run around scattering my genes all over your shiny new world. That's a promise."

"Your appeal is rejected," came the inflexible reply.

Al shrugged. He knew when he was beaten. "Okay," he said wearily. "I didn't want to live in your damn century anyway. When's the execution?"

"*Execution*?" Spadebeard looked stunned. "Dove's whiskers, do you think we would—would actually—"

He couldn't get the word out.

Al supplied it: "Put me to death?"

Spadebeard's expression was sickly. He looked ready to retch. Al heard him mutter vehemently to his companions in the observation cubicle: "Gonnim def larrimog! Egfar!"

"Murrifar althrosk," suggested one of his companions.

Spadebeard, evidently reassured, nodded. He said to Al, "No doubt a barbarian like yourself *would* expect to be—to be made dead." Gulping, he went gamely on. "We have no such vindictive intention."

"Well, what *are* you going to do to me?"

"Send you across the timeline to a world where your friends, the mutated ones, reign supreme," Spadebeard replied. "It's the least we can do for you, spy."

The hidden door of his cell puckered open. Another armor-suited figure entered, pointing a gun, and discharged a blob of blue light that drifted toward Al and rapidly englobed him. He was drawn by the trailing end out into a corridor.

It hadn't been a very sociable reception here in the twenty-fifth century, he thought as he was tugged along the hallway. In a way, he couldn't blame them. A time-traveler from the past was bound to be laden down with all sorts of germs. They couldn't risk letting him run around *breathing* at everybody. No wonder that crowd of onlookers had panicked when he had opened his mouth to speak to them.

The other business, though, that of his being a spy for the mutants—he couldn't figure that out at all. If the mutants had been wiped out fifty years ago, why worry about spies now? At least his species had managed to defeat the underground organization of potbellied little men. That was comforting. He wished he could get back to 1959, if only to snap his fingers in their jowly faces and tell them that all their sinister scheming was going to come to nothing.

Where was he heading now? Spadebeard had said, *Across the timeline to a world where the mutated ones reign supreme.* Whatever across the timeline meant, Al thought.

He was ushered into an impressive laboratory room and, bubble and all, was thrust into the waiting clasps of something that looked depressingly like an electric chair. Brisk technicians bustled around, throwing switches and checking connections.

Al glanced in appeal at Spadebeard. "Will you tell me what's going on?"

"It is very difficult to express in medieval terms," the linguist said. "The device makes use of dollibar force to transmit you through an inverse dormin vector—do I make myself clear?"

"Not very," Al confessed.

"Unhelpable. But you understand the concept of parallel continua at least, of course."

"No."

"Does it mean anything to you if I say that you'll be shunted across the spokes of the time-wheel to a totality that is simultaneously parallel and tangent to our four-space?"

"That isn't much better," Al said resignedly, for all he was really getting was a headache. "You might as well start shunting me, I suppose."

Spadebeard nodded and turned to a technician. "Vorstrar althrosk," he commanded.

"Murrifar."

The technician grabbed an immense toggle switch with both hands and groaningly dragged it shut. Al heard a brief whine of closing relays. Then darkness surrounded him.

Once again he found himself on a city street. But the pavement was cracked and buckled, and grassblades poked up through the neglected concrete.

A dry voice said, "All right, you. Don't sprawl there like a ninny. Get up and come along."

Al peered doubtfully up into the snout of a fair-sized pistol of enormous caliber. It was held by a short, fat, baldheaded man. Four identical companions stood near him with arms folded. They all looked very much like Mordecai, Waldemar, Giovanni, and the rest, except that these mutants were decked out in futuristic-looking costumes bright with flashy gold trim and rocketship insignia.

Al put up his hands. "Where am I?" he asked in confusion.

"Earth, of course. You've just come through a dimensional gateway from the continuum of the Normals. Come along, spy. Into the van."

"But I'm not a spy," Al mumbled without much hope as the five little men bundled him into a blue and red car the size of a small yacht. "At least, I'm not spying on *you*. I mean—"

"Save the explanations for the Overlord," was the curt instruction.

Al huddled miserably cramped between two vigilant mutants, while the others sat behind him. The van moved seemingly of its own volition, and at an enormous rate. A mutant power, Al thought. After a while he said, "Could you at least tell me what year this is?"

"Yes—2431," snapped the mutant to his left.

"But that's the same year it was over *there*."

"Certainly. What else could it be?"

The question floored Al. He was silent for perhaps half a mile more. Since the van had no windows, he stared morosely at his feet.

Finally he asked, "How come you aren't afraid of catching my germs then? Over back of—ah—the dimensional gateway, they kept me cooped up in a force-field all the time so I wouldn't contaminate them. But you go right ahead breathing the same air I do."

"Do you think we fear the germs of a Normal, spy?" sneered the mutant at Al's right. "You forget that we're a superior race."

Al nodded. "Yes. I forgot about that."

The van halted suddenly and the mutant police hustled Al out, past a crowd of peering little fat men and women, and into a colossal dome of a building whose exterior was covered completely with faceted green glass. The effect was one of massive ugliness.

They ushered him into a sort of throne room presided over by a mutant fatter than the rest. The policeman gripping Al's right arm hissed, "Bow when you enter the presence of the Overlord."

Al wasn't minded to argue. He dropped to his knees along with the others. A booming voice from above rang out. "What have you brought me today?"

"A spy, Your Nobility."

"Another? Rise, spy."

Al rose. "Begging Your Nobility's pardon, I'd like to put in a word or two on my own behalf—"

"Silence!" the Overlord roared.

Al closed his mouth.

The mutant drew himself up to his full height, about

five feet one, and said, "The Normals have sent you across the dimensional gulf to spy on us."

"No, Your Nobility. They were afraid I'd spy on *them*, so they sent me over here. I'm from the year 1959, you see." Briefly, he explained everything, beginning with the bollixed phone call and ending with his capture by the Overlord's men a short while ago.

The Overlord looked skeptical. "It is well known that the Normals plan to cross the dimensional gulf from their phantom world to this, the real one, and invade our civilization. You're but the latest of their advance scouts. Admit it!"

"No, Your Nobility, I'm not. On the other side, they told me I was a spy from 1959, and now you say I'm a spy from the other dimension. But I tell you—"

"Enough!" the mutant leader thundered. "Take him away. Place him in custody. We shall decide his fate later!"

Someone else already occupied the cell into which Al was thrust. He was a lanky, sad-faced Normal who slouched forward to shake hands once the door had clanged shut.

"Thurizad manifosk," he said.

"Sorry, I don't speak that language," said Al.

The other grinned. "I understand. All right: greetings. I'm Darren Phelp. Are you a spy too?"

"No, dammit!" Al snapped. Then: "Sorry. Didn't mean to take it out on you. My name's Al Miller. Are you a native of this place?"

"Me? Dove's whiskers, what a sense of humor! Of course I'm not a native! You know as well as I do that there aren't any Normals left in this fourspace continuum."

"None at all?"

"Hasn't been one born here in centuries," Phelp said. "But you're just joking, eh? You're from Baileffod's outfit, I suppose."

"Who?"

"Baileffod. *Baileffod!* You mean you aren't? Then you must be from higher up!" Phelp thrust his hands sideways in some kind of gesture of respect. "Penguin's paws, Excellency, I apologize. I should have seen at once—"

"No, I'm not from your organization at all," Al said. "I don't know what you're talking about. Word of honor."

Phelp smiled cunningly. "Of *course*, Excellency! I understand completely."

"Cut that out! Why doesn't anyone ever believe me? I'm not from Baileffod and I'm not from higher up. I come from 1959. Do you hear me—1959? And that's the truth."

Phelp's eyes went wide. "From the *past?*"

Al nodded. "I stumbled into the mutants in 1959 and they shipped me five centuries ahead to get rid of me. Only when I arrived, I wasn't welcome, so I was shipped across the dimensional whatzis to here. Everyone thinks I'm a spy, wherever I go. What are you doing here?"

Phelp smiled. "Why, I *am* a spy."

"From 2431?"

"Naturally. We have to keep tabs on the mutants somehow. I came through the gateway wearing an invisibility shield, but it popped an ultrone and I vizzed out. They jugged me last month and I suppose I'm stuck in this place for keeps."

Al rubbed thumbs tiredly against his eyeballs. "Wait a minute—how come you speak my language? On the other side, they had to get hold of a linguistics expert to talk to me."

"All spies are trained to talk English," said Phelp. "That's the language the mutants speak here. In the real world, we speak Vorkish, naturally. It's the language developed by the Normals for communication during the Mutant Wars. Your 'linquistics expert' was probably one of our top spies."

"And over here the mutants have won?"

"Completely. Three hundred years ago, in this continuum, the mutants developed a two-way time machine that enabled them to go back and forth, eliminating Normal leaders before they were born. Whereas in our world, the *real* world, two-way time travel is impossible. That's where the continuum split begins. We Normals fought a grim war of extermination against the mutants in our fourspace and finally wiped them out, despite their superior powers, in 2390. Clear?"

"More or less." Rather less than more, Al added privately. "So there are only mutants in this world, and there are only Normals in your world."

"Exactly!"

"And you're a spy from the other side."

"You've got it now! You see, even though, strictly speaking, this world is only a phantom, it's got some pretty real characteristics. For instance, if the mutants killed you here, you'd be dead. Permanently. So there's a lot of rivalry across the gateway; the mutants are always scheming to invade us, and vice versa. Confidentially, I don't think anything will ever come of all the scheming."

"You don't?"

"Nah," Phelp said. "The way things stand now, each side has a perfectly good enemy just beyond reach. But actually going to war would be messy, while relaxing our guard and allowing peace to break out would foul up our economy. So we keep sending spies back and forth, and prepare for war. It's a nice system, except when you happen to get yourself caught, like me."

"What'll happen to you?"

Phelp shrugged. "They may let me rot here for a few decades. Or they might decide to condition me and send me back as a spy for *them*. Tiger tails, who could know?"

"Would you change sides like that?"

"I wouldn't have any choice—not after I was conditioned," Phelp said. "But I don't worry much about it. It's a risk I knew about when I signed on for spy duty."

Al shuddered. It was beyond him how someone could voluntarily let himself get involved in this game of dimension shifting and mutant battling. But it takes all sorts to make a continuum, he philosophically decided.

Half an hour later, three rotund mutant police came to fetch him. They marched him downstairs and into a bare, ugly little room where a battery of interrogators quizzed him for better than an hour. He stuck to his story, throughout everything, until at last they indicated they were through with him.

He spent the next two hours in a drafty cell, by himself, until finally a gaudily robed mutant unlocked the door and said, "The Overlord commands you to present yourself."

The Overlord looked worried. He leaned forward on his throne, fist digging into his fleshy chin. In his booming voice—Al realized at last that it was artificially amplified—the Overlord rumbled, "Miller, you're a *problem*."

"I'm sorry, Your Nobil—"

"*Quiet!* I'll do the talking."

Al did not reply.

The Overlord went on, "We've checked your story in-side and out, and confirmed it with one of our spies on the other side of the gate. You really are from 1959, or thereabouts. What can we do with you? Generally speak-ing, when we catch a Normal snooping around here, we psycho-condition him and send him back across the gate-way to spy for us. But we can't do that to you, because you don't belong on the other side, and they've already tossed you out once. On the other hand, we can't keep you here, maintaining you forever at state expense. And it wouldn't be civilized to kill you, would it?"

"No, Your Nobil—"

"*Silence!*"

Al gulped.

The Overlord glowered at him and continued thinking out loud. "I suppose we could perform experiments on you, though. You must be a walking laboratory of Normal microorganisms that we could synthesize and fire through the gateway when we invade their fourspace. Yes, by the Grome, *then* you'd be useful to our cause! Zechariah?"

"Yes, Nobility?" a ribbon-bedecked guardsman snapped to attention.

"Take this Normal to the biological laboratories for examination. I'll have further instructions as soon as—"

Al heard a peculiar whanging noise from the back of the throne room. The Overlord appeared to freeze on his throne. Turning, Al saw a band of determined-looking Normals come bursting in, led by Darren Phelp.

"*There* you are!" Phelp cried. "I've been looking all over for you!" He was waving a peculiar needle-nozzled gun.

"What's going on?" Al gasped.

Phelp grinned. "The invasion! It came, after all! Our

troops are pouring through the gateway armed with these freezer guns. They immobilize any mutant who gets in the way of the field."

"When—when did all this happen?"

"It started two hours ago. We've captured the entire city! Come on, will you? Whiskers, there's no time to waste!"

"Where in blazes am I supposed to go?"

Phelp smiled. "To the nearest dimensional lab, of course. We're going to send you back to your own time."

A dozen triumphant Normals stood in a tense knot around Al in the laboratory. From outside came the sound of jubilant singing. The invasion was a howling success.

As Phelp explained it, the victory was due to the recent invention of a kind of time-barrier projector. The projector had cut off all contact between the mutant world and its own future, preventing time-traveling mutant scouts from getting back to 2431 with news of the invasion. With two-way travel, the great mutant advantage, thus nullified, the success of the surprise attack was made possible—and easy.

Al listened to this explanation with minimal interest. He barely understood every third word, and, in any event, his main concern was in getting home.

He was strapped into a streamlined and much modified version of the temporal centrifuge that had originally hurled him forward into 2431.

Phelp explained things to him. "You see here, we set the machine for 1959. What day was it when you left? And how close can you get to the moment?"

"Ah—October tenth. It was exactly three thirty in the afternoon."

"Make the setting, Frozz." Phelp nodded. "You'll be

shunted back along the timeline. Of course, you'll land in this continuum, since in our world there's no such thing as pastward time travel. But once you reach your own time, all you do is activate this small transdimensional generator, and you'll be hurled across safe and sound into the very day you left, in your own fourspace."

"You can't know how much I appreciate all this," Al said very warmly.

He felt a pleasant glow of love for all mankind, for the first time since his unhappy phone call. At last someone was taking sympathetic interest in his plight. At last he was on his way home, back to the relative sanity of 1959, where he could start forgetting this entire nightmarish jaunt. Mutants and Normals and spies and time machines. . . .

"You'd better get going," Phelp said. "We have to get the occupation under way here."

"Sure," Al agreed. "Don't let me hold you up. I can't wait to get going—no offense intended."

"And remember, soon as your surroundings look familiar, jab the activator button on this generator. Otherwise you'll slither into an interspace where we couldn't answer for the consequences."

Al nodded tensely. "I won't forget."

"I hope not. Ready?"

"Ready."

Someone threw a switch. Al began to spin. He heard the popping sound that was the rupturing of the temporal matrix. Like a cork shot from a champagne bottle, Al arched out backward through time, heading for 1959.

He woke in his own room on 23rd Street. His head hurt. His mind was full of phrases like temporal centrifuge and transdimensional generator.

He picked himself off the floor and rubbed his head.

Wow, he thought. It must have been a sudden fainting spell. And now his head was crowded with nonsense.

Going to the sideboard, he pulled out the half-empty bourbon bottle and measured off a few fingers' worth.

After the drink, his nerves felt steadier. His mind was still cluttered with inexplicable thoughts and images. Sinister little fat men and complex machines, transparent roadways in the air and men in fancy tunics.

A bad dream, he thought.

Then he remembered. It wasn't any dream. He had actually taken the round trip into 2431, returning by way of some other continuum.

He had pressed the generator button at the proper time, and now here he was, safe and sound. No longer the football of a bunch of different factions. Home in his own snug little fourspace, or whatever it was.

He frowned. He recalled that Mordecai had severed the telephone wire. But the phone looked intact now. Maybe it had been fixed while he was gone. He picked it up. Unless he got that loan extension today, he was cooked.

There was no need for him to look up the number of the Friendly Finance Corporation; he knew it all too well. He began to dial. MUrray Hill 4—

The receiver clicked queerly. A voice said, "Come in, Operator Nine. Operator Nine, do you read me?"

Al's jaw sagged. This is where I came in, he thought wildly. He struggled to put down the phone. But his muscles would not respond. It would be easier to bend the sun in its orbit than to break the path of the continuum. He heard his own voice say, "I didn't want the operator. There must be something wrong with my phone if—"

"Just a minute. Who *are* you?"

Al fought to break the contact. But he was hemmed

away in a small corner of his mind while his voice went on, "I ought to ask you that. What are you doing on the other end, anyway? I hadn't even finished dialing. I got as far as MU-four and—"

"Well? You dialed MUgwump four and you got us. What more do you want?" A suspicious pause. "Say, you aren't Operator Nine!"

Inwardly, Al wanted to scream. No scream would come. In this continuum, the past (his future) was immutable. He was caught on the track, and there was no escape. None whatever. And, he realized in frozen horror, there never would be.

To the Dark Star

···➤◉◄···

WE CAME to the dark star, the microcephalon and
the adapted girl, and I, and our struggle began. A poorly
assorted lot we were, to begin with. The mircocephalon
hailed from Quendar IV, where they grow their people
with greasy gray skins, looming shoulders, and virtually no
heads at all. He—it—was wholly alien, at least. The girl
was not, and so I hated her.

She came from a world in the Procyon system, where
the air was more or less Earth-type, but the gravity was
double ours. There were other differences, too. She was
thick through the shoulders, thick through the waist, a
block of flesh. The genetic surgeons had begun with human raw material, but they had transformed it into something nearly as alien as the microcephalon. Nearly.

We were a scientific team, so they said. Sent out to observe the last moments of a dying star. A great interstellar effort. Pick three specialists at random, put them in a ship, hurl them halfway across the universe to observe what man had never observed before. A fine idea. Noble. Inspiring. We knew our subject well. We were ideal.

But we felt no urge to cooperate, because we hated one another.

The adapted girl—Miranda—was at the controls the day that the dark star actually came into sight. She spent hours studying it before she deigned to let us know that we were at our destination. Then she buzzed us out of our quarters.

I entered the scanning room. Miranda's muscular bulk overflowed the glossy chair before the main screen. The microcephalon stood beside her, a squat figure on a tripod-like arrangement of bony legs, the great shoulders hunched and virtually concealing the tiny cupola of the head. There was no real reason why an organism's brain *had* to be in its skull, and not safely tucked away in the thorax; but I had never grown accustomed to the sight of the creature. I fear I have little tolerance for aliens.

"Look," Miranda said, and the screen glowed.

The dark star hung in dead center, at a distance of perhaps eight light-days—as close as we dared to come. It was not quite dead, and not quite dark. I stared in awe. It was a huge thing, some four solar masses, the imposing remnant of a gigantic star. On the screen there glowed what looked like an enormous lava field. Islands of ash and slag the size of worlds drifted in a sea of molten and glowing magma. A dull red illumination burnished the screen. Black against crimson, the ruined star still throbbed with ancient power. In the depths of that monstrous slagheap compressed nuclei groaned and gasped.

Once the radiance of this star had lit a solar system; but I did not dare think of the billions of years that had passed since then, nor of the possible civilizations that had hailed the source of all light and warmth before the catastrophe.

Miranda said, "I've picked up the thermals already. The surface temperature averages about nine hundred degrees. There's no chance of the landing."

I scowled at her. "What good is the *average* temperature? Get a specific. One of those islands—"

"The ash masses are radiating at two hundred and fifty degrees. The interstices go from one thousand degrees on up. Everything works out to a mean of nine hundred degrees, and you'd melt in an instant if you went down there. You're welcome to go, brother. With my blessing."

"I didn't say—"

"You implied that there'd be a safe place to land on that fireball," Miranda snapped. Her voice was a basso boom; there was plenty of resonance space in that vast chest of hers. "You snidely cast doubt on my ability to—"

"We will use the crawler to make our inspection," said the microcephalon in its reasonable way. "There never was any plan to make a physical landing on the star."

Miranda subsided. I stared in awe at the sight that filled our screen.

A star takes a long time to die, and the relict I viewed impressed me with its colossal age. It had blazed for billions of years, until the hydrogen that was its fuel had at last been exhausted, and its thermonuclear furnace started to sputter and go out. A star has defenses against growing cold; as its fuel supply dwindles, it begins to contract, raising its density and converting gravitational potential energy into thermal energy. It takes on new life; now a white dwarf, with a density of tons per cubic inch, it burns in a stable way until at last it grows dark.

We have studied white dwarfs for centuries, and we know their secrets—so we think. A cup of matter from a white dwarf now orbits the observatory on Pluto for our further illumination.

But the star of our screen was different.

It had once been a large star—greater than the Chandrasekhar limit, 1.2 solar masses. Thus it was not content to shrink step by step to the status of a white dwarf. The stellar core grew so dense that catastrophe came before stability; when it had converted all its hydrogen to iron-56, it fell into catastrophic collapse and went supernova. A shock wave ran through the core, converting the kinetic energy of collapse into heat. Neutrinos spewed outward; the envelope of the star reached temperatures upwards of 200 billion degrees; thermal energy became intense radiation, streaming away from the agonized star and shedding the luminosity of a galaxy for a brief, fitful moment.

What we beheld now was the core left behind by the supernova explosion. Even after that awesome fury, what was intact was of great mass. The shattered hulk had been cooling for eons, cooling toward the final death. For a small star, that death would be the simple death of coldness: the ultimate burnout, the black dwarf drifting through the void like a hideous mound of ash, lightless, without warmth. But this, our stellar core, was still beyond the Chandrasekhar limit. A special death was reserved for it, a weird and improbable death.

And that was why we had come to watch it perish, the microcephalon and the adapted girl and I.

I parked our small vessel in an orbit that gave the dark star plenty of room. Miranda busied herself with her measurements and computations. The microcephalon had more abstruse things to do. The work was well divided; we each had our chores. The expense of sending a ship so great a distance had necessarily limited the size of the expedition. Three of us: a representative of the basic human stock, a representative of the adapted colonists, a representative of the race of microcephalons, the Quendar people, the only other intelligent beings in the known universe.

Three dedicated scientists. And therefore three who would live in serene harmony during the course of the work, since as everyone knows scientists have no emotions and think only of their professional mysteries. As everyone knows. When did that myth start to circulate, anyway?

I said to Miranda, "Where are the figures for radial oscillation?"

She replied, "See my report. It'll be published early next year in—"

"Damn you, are you doing that deliberately? I need those figures now!"

"Give me your totals on the mass-density curve, then."

"They aren't ready. All I've got is raw data."

"That's a lie! The computer's been running for days! I've seen it," she boomed at me.

I was ready to leap at her throat. It would have been a mighty battle; her 300-pound body was not trained for personal combat as mine was, but she had all the advantages of strength and size. Could I club her in some vital place before she broke me in half? I weighed my options.

Then the microcephalon appeared and made peace once more, with a few feather-soft words.

Only the alien among us seemed to conform at all to the stereotype of that emotionless abstraction, "the scientist." It was not true, of course; for all we could tell, the microcephalon seethed with jealousies and lusts and angers, but we had no clue to their outward manifestation. Its voice was as flat as a vocoder transmission. The creature moved peacefully among us, the mediator between Miranda and me. I despised it for its mask of tranquility. I suspected, too, that the microcephalon loathed the two of us for our willingness to vent our emotions, and took a sadistic pleasure from asserting superiority by calming us.

We returned to our research. We still had some time before the last collapse of the dark star.

It had cooled nearly to death. Now there was still some thermonuclear activity within that bizarre core, enough to keep the star too warm for an actual landing. It was radiating primarily in the optical band of the spectrum, and by stellar standards its temperature was nil, but for us it would be like prowling the heart of a live volcano.

Finding the star had been a chore. Its luminosity was so low that it could not be detected optically at a greater distance than a light-month or so; it had been spotted by a satellite-borne X-ray telescope that had detected the emanations of the degenerate neutron gas of the core. Now we gathered round and performed our functions of measurement. We recorded things like neutron drip and electron capture. We computed the time remaining before the final collapse. Where necessary, we collaborated; most of the time we went our separate ways. The tension aboard ship was nasty. Miranda went out of her way to provoke me. And, though I like to think that I was beyond and above her beastliness, I have to confess that I matched her, obstruction for obstruction. Our alien companion never made any overt attempt to annoy us; but indirect aggression can be maddening in close quarters, and the microcephalon's benign indifference to us was as potent a force for dissonance as Miranda's outright shrewishness or my own deliberately mulish responses.

The star hung in our viewscreen, bubbling with vitality that belied its dying state. The islands of slag, thousands of miles in diameter, broke free and drifted at random on the sea of inner flame. Now and then spouting eruptions of stripped particles came heaving up out of the core. Our figures showed that the final collapse was drawing near, and that meant that an awkward choice was upon us. Someone was going to have to monitor the last moments of the dark star. The risks were high. It could be fatal.

None of us mentioned that ultimate responsibility.

We moved toward the climax of our work. Miranda continued to annoy me in every way, sheerly for the devilishness of it. How I hated her! We had begun this voyage coolly, with nothing dividing us but professional jealousy. But the months of proximity had turned our quarrel into a personal feud. The mere sight of her maddened me, and I'm sure she reacted the same way. She devoted her energies to an immature attempt to trouble me. Lately she took to walking around the ship in the nude, I suspect trying to stir some spark of sexual feeling in me that she could douse with a blunt, mocking refusal. The trouble was that I could feel no desire whatever for a grotesque adapted creature like Miranda, a mound of muscle and bone twice my size. The sight of her massive udders and monumental buttocks stirred nothing in me but disgust.

The witch! Was it desire she was trying to kindle by exposing herself that way, or loathing? Either way, she had me. She must have known that.

In our third month in orbit around the dark star, the microcephalon announced, "The coordinates show an approach to the Schwarzschild radius. It is time to send our vehicle to the surface of the star."

"Which one of us rides monitor?" I asked.

Miranda's beefy hand shot out at me. "You do."

"I think you're better equipped to make the observations," I told her sweetly.

"Thank you, no."

"We must draw lots," said the microcephalon.

"Unfair," said Miranda. She glared at me. "He'll do something to rig the odds. I couldn't trust him."

"How else can we choose?" the alien asked.

"We can vote," I suggested. "I nominate Miranda."

"I nominate him," she snapped.

The microcephalon put his ropy tentacles across the tiny nodule of skull between his shoulders. "Since I do not choose to nominate myself," he said mildly, "it falls to me to make a deciding choice between the two of you. I refuse the responsibility. Another method must be found."

We let the matter drop for the moment. We still had a few more days before the critical time was at hand.

With all my heart I wished Miranda into the monitor capsule. It would mean at best her death, at worst a sober muting of her abrasive personality, if she were the one who sat in vicariously on the throes of the dark star. I was willing to stop at nothing to give her that remarkable and demolishing experience.

What was going to happen to our star may sound strange to a layman; but the theory had been outlined by Einstein and Schwarzschild a thousand years ago, and had been confirmed many times, though never until our expedition had it been observed at close range. When matter reaches a sufficiently high density, it can force the local curvature of space to close around itself, forming a pocket isolated from the rest of the universe. A collapsing super-nova core creates just such a Schwarzschild singularity. After it has cooled to near-zero temperature, a core of the proper Chandrasekhar mass undergoes a violent collapse to zero volume, simultaneously attaining an infinite density.

In a way, it swallows itself and vanishes from this universe—for how could the fabric of the continuum tolerate a point of infinite density and zero volume?

Such collapses are rare. Most stars come to a state of cold equilibrium and remain there. We were on the threshold of a singularity, and we were in a position to put an observer vehicle right on the surface of the cold star, sending back an exact description of the events up until the final moment when the collapsing core broke through the walls of the universe and disappeared.

Someone had to ride gain on the equipment, though. Which meant, in effect, vicariously participating in the death of the star. We had learned in other cases that it becomes difficult for the monitor to distinguish between reality and effect; he accepts the sensory percepts from the distant pickup as his own experience. A kind of psychic backlash results; often, an unwary brain is burned out entirely.

What impact would the direct experience of being crushed out of existence in a singularity have on a monitoring observer?

I was eager to find out. But not with myself as the sacrificial victim.

I cast about for some way to get Miranda into that capsule. She, of course, was doing the same for me. It was she who made her move first by attempting to drug me into compliance.

What drug she used, I have no idea. Her people are fond of the nonaddictive hallucinogens, which help them break the monotony of their stark, oversized world. Somehow Miranda interfered with the programming of my food supply and introduced one of her pet alkaloids. I began to feel the effects an hour after I had eaten. I walked to the screen to study the surging mass of the dark star—much changed from its appearance of only a few months before—and as I looked, the image in the screen began to swirl and melt, and tongues of flame did an eerie dance along the horizons of the star.

I clung to the rail. Sweat broke from my pores. Was the ship liquefying? The floor heaved and bucked beneath me. I looked at the back of my hand and saw continents of ash set in a grouting of fiery magma.

Miranda stood behind me. "Come with me to the capsule," she murmured. "The monitor's ready for launching now. You'll find it wonderful to see the last moments."

Lurching after her, I padded through the strangely altered ship. Miranda's adapted form was even more alien than usual; her musculature rippled and flowed, her golden hair held all the colors of the spectrum, her flesh was oddly puckered and cratered, with wiry filaments emerging from the skin. I felt quite calm about entering the capsule. She slid back the hatch, revealing the gleaming console of the panel within, and I began to enter, and then suddenly the hallucination deepened and I saw in the darkness of the capsule a devil beyond all imagination.

I dropped to the floor and lay there twitching.

Miranda seized me. To her I was no more than a doll. She lifted me, began to thrust me into the capsule. Perspiration soaked me. Reality returned. I slipped from her grasp and wriggled away, rolling toward the bulkhead.

Like a beast of primordial forests she came ponderously after me.

"No," I said. "I won't go."

She halted. Her face twisted in anger, and she turned away from me in defeat. I lay panting and quivering until my mind was purged of phantoms. It had been close.

It was my turn a short while later. Fight force with force, I told myself. I could not risk more of Miranda's treachery. Time was running short.

From our surgical kit I took a hypnoprobe used for anesthesia, and rigged it in series with one of Miranda's telescope antennae. Programming it for induction of docility, I left it to go to work on her. When she made her observations, the hypnoprobe would purr its siren song of sinister coaxing, and—perhaps—Miranda would bend to my wishes.

It did not work.

I watched her going to her telescopes. I saw her broad-beamed form settling in place. In my mind I heard the hypnoprobe's gentle whisper, as I knew it must sound to Miranda. It was telling her to relax, to obey. "The capsule . . . get into the capsule . . . you will monitor the crawler . . . you . . . you . . . you will do it. . . . "

I waited for her to arise and move like a sleepwalker to the waiting capsule. Her tawny body was motionless. Muscles rippled beneath that obscenely bare flesh. The probe had her! Yes! It was getting to her!

No.

She clawed at the telescope as though it were a steel-tipped wasp drilling for her brain. The barrel recoiled, and she pushed herself away from it, whirling around. Her eyes glowed with rage. Her enormous body reared up before me. She seemed half berserk. The probe had had some effect on her; I could see her dizzied strides, and knew that she was awry. But it had not been potent enough. Something within that adapted brain of hers gave her the strength to fight off the murky shroud of hypnotism.

"You did that!" she roared. "You gimmicked the telescope, didn't you?"

"I don't know what you mean, Miranda."

"Liar! Fraud! Sneak!"

"Calm down. You're rocking us out of orbit."

"I'll rock all I want! What was that thing that had its fingers in my brain? You put it there! What was it, the hypnoprobe you used?"

"Yes," I admitted coolly. "And what was it you put into my food? Which hallucinogen?"

"It didn't work."

"Neither did my hypnoprobe. Miranda, someone's got to get into that capsule. In a few hours we'll be at the critical point. We don't dare come back without the essential observations. Make the sacrifice."

"For *you*?"

"For science," I said, appealing to that noble abstraction.

I got the horselaugh I deserved. Then Miranda strode toward me. She had recovered her coordination in full, now, and it seemed as though she were planning to thrust me into the capsule by main force. Her ponderous arms enfolded me. The stink of her thickened hide made me retch. I felt ribs creaking within me. I hammered at her body, searching for the pressure points that would drop her in a felled heap. We punished each other cruelly, grunting back and forth across the cabin. It was a fierce contest of skill against mass. She would not fall, and I would not crush.

The toneless buzz of the microcephalon said, "Release each other. The collapsing star is nearing its Schwarzschild radius. We must act now."

Miranda's arms slipped away from me. I stepped back, glowering at her, to suck breath into my battered body. Livid bruises were appearing on her skin. We had come to a mutual awareness of mutual strength; but the capsule still was empty. Hatred hovered like a globe of ball lightning between us. The gray, greasy alien creature stood to one side.

I would not care to guess which of us had the idea first, Miranda or I. But we moved swiftly. The microcephalon scarcely murmured a word of protest as we hustled it down the passage and into the room that held the capsule. Miranda was smiling. I felt relief. She held the alien tight while I opened the hatch, and then she thrust it through. We dogged the hatch together.

"Launch the crawler," she said.

I nodded and went to the controls. Like a dart from a blowgun the crawler housing was expelled from our ship and journeyed under high acceleration to the surface of the dark star. It contained a compact vehicle with sturdy jointed legs, controlled by remote pickup from the observation capsule aboard ship. As the observer moved arms and feet within the control harnesses, servo relays actuated the hydraulic pistons in the crawler, eight light-days away. It moved in parallel response, clambering over the slagheaps of a solar surface that no organic life could endure.

The microcephalon operated the crawler with skill. We watched through the shielded video pickups, getting a close-range view of that inferno. Even a cold sun is more terrifyingly hot than any planet of man.

The signals coming from the star altered with each

moment, as the full force of the red-shift gripped the fading light. Something unutterably strange was taking place down there; and the mind of our microcephalon was rooted to the scene. Tidal gravitational forces lashed the star. The crawler was lifted, heaved, compressed, subjected to strains that slowly ripped it apart. The alien witnessed it all, and dictated an account of what he saw, slowly, methodically, without a flicker of fear.

The singularity approached. The tidal forces aspired toward infinity. The microcephalon sounded bewildered at last as it attempted to describe the topological phenomena that no eye had seen before. Infinite density, zero volume— how did the mind comprehend it? The crawler was contorted into an inconceivable shape; and yet its sensors obstinately continued to relay data, filtered through the mind of the microcephalon and into our computer banks.

Then came silence. Our screens went dead. The unthinkable had at last occurred, and the dark star had passed within the radius of singularity. It had collapsed into oblivion, taking with it the crawler. To the alien in the observation capsule aboard our ship, it was as though he too had vanished into that pocket of hyperspace that passed all understanding.

I looked toward the heavens. The dark star was gone. Our detectors picked up the outpouring of energy that marked its annihilation. We were buffeted briefly on the wave of force that ripped outward from the place where the star had been, and then all was calm.

Miranda and I exchanged glances.

"Let the microcephalon out," I said.

She opened the hatch. The alien sat quite calmly at the control console. It did not speak. Miranda assisted it from the capsule. Its eyes were expressionless; but they had never shown anything, anyway.

We are on our way back to the worlds of our galaxy, now. The mission has been accomplished. We have relayed priceless and unique data.

The microcephalon has not spoken since we removed it from the capsule. I do not believe it will speak again.

Miranda and I perform our chores in harmony. The hostility between us is gone. We are partners in crime, now, edgy with guilt that we do not admit to one another. We tend our shipmate with loving care.

Someone had to make the observations, after all. There were no volunteers. The situation called for force, or the deadlock would never have been broken.

But Miranda and I hated each other, you say? Why, then, should we cooperate?

We both are humans, Miranda and I. The microcephalon is not. In the end, that made the difference. In the last analysis, Miranda and I decided that we humans must stick together. There are ties that bind.

We speed onward toward civilization.

She smiles at me. I do not find her hateful now. The microcephalon is silent.

Neighbor

---◦---

I

FRESH SNOW had fallen during the night. Now it lay like a white sheet atop the older snow, nine or ten feet of it, that already covered the plain. Now all was smooth and clear almost to the horizon. As Michael Holt peered through the foot-thick safety glass of his command room window, he saw, first of all, the zone of brown earth, a hundred yards in diameter, circling his house, and then the beginning of the snowfield with a few jagged bare trees jutting through it, and then, finally, a blot on the horizon, the metallic tower that was Andrew McDermott's dwelling.

Not in seventy or eighty years had Holt looked at the McDermott place without feeling hatred and irritation. The planet was big enough, wasn't it? Why had McDermott chosen to stick his pile of misshapen steel down right where Holt had to look at it all his days? McDermott's estate was big enough. McDermott could have built his house another fifty or sixty miles to the east, near the banks of the wide, shallow river that flowed through the heart of the continent. He hadn't cared to. Holt had politely suggested it, when the surveyors and architects first came out from Earth. McDermott had just as politely insisted on putting his house where he wanted to put it.

It was still there. Michael Holt peered at it, and his insides roiled. He walked to the control console of the armament panel, and let his thin, gnarled hands rest for a moment on a gleaming rheostat.

There was an almost sexual manner to the way Holt fondled the jutting knobs and studs of the console. Now that his two hundredth year was approaching, he rarely handled the bodies of his wives that way any more. But then he did not love his wives as keenly as he loved the artillery emplacement with which he could blow Andrew McDermott to atoms.

Just let him provoke me, Holt thought.

He stood by the panel, a tall, gaunt man with a withered face and a savage hook of a nose and a surprisingly thick shock of faded red hair. He closed his eyes and allowed himself the luxury of a daydream.

He imagined that Andrew McDermott had given him offense. Not simply the eternal offense of being there in his view, but some direct, specific affront. Poaching on his land, perhaps. Or sending a robot out to hack down a tree on the borderland. Or putting up a flashing neon sign that mocked Holt in some vulgar way. Anything that would serve as an excuse for hostilities.

And then: Holt saw himself coming up here to the

command room and broadcasting an ultimatum to the enemy. "Take that sign down, McDermott," he might say. "Keep your robots off my land," perhaps. Or else, "This means war!"

McDermott would answer with a blast of radiation, of course, because that was the kind of sneak he was. The deflector screens of Holt's front line defenses would handle the bolt with ease, soaking it in and feeding the energy straight to Holt's own generators.

Then, at long last, Holt would answer back. His fingers would tighten on the controls. Crackling arcs of energy would leap toward the ionosphere and bound downward at McDermott's place, spearing through his pitiful screens as though they weren't there. Holt saw himself gripping the controls with knuckle-whitening fervor, launching thunderbolt after thunderbolt while on the horizon Andrew McDermott's hideous keep blazed and glowed in hellish fire and crumpled and toppled and ran in molten puddles over the snow.

Yes, that would be the moment to live for!

That would be the moment of triumph!

To step back from the controls at last, and look through the window and see the glowing red spot on the horizon where the McDermott place had been. To pat the controls as though they were the flanks of a beloved old horse. To leave the house, and ride across the borderland into the McDermott estate, and see the charred ruin, and know that he was gone forever.

Then, of course, there would be an inquiry. The fifty lords of the planet would meet to discuss the battle, and Holt would explain, "He wantonly provoked me. I need not tell you how he gave me offense by building his house within my view. But this time—"

And Holt's fellow lords would nod sagely. They would understand, for they valued their own unblemished views as highly as Holt himself. They would exonerate him and grant him McDermott's land, as far as the horizon, so no newcomer could repeat the offense.

Michael Holt smiled. The daydream left him satisfied. His heart raced perhaps a little too enthusiastically as he pictured that slagheap on the horizon. He made an effort to calm himself. He was, after all, a fragile old man, much as he hated to admit it, and even the excitement of a daydream taxed his strength.

He walked away from the panel, back to the window. Nothing had changed. The zone of brown earth where his melters kept back the snow, and then the white field, and finally the excrescence on the horizon, glinting coppery red in the thin midday sunlight. Holt scowled. The daydream had changed nothing. No shot had been fired. McDermott's keep still stained the view. Turning, Holt began to shuffle slowly out of the room, toward the dropshaft that would take him five floors downward to his family.

II

The communicator chimed. Holt stared at the screen in surprise.

"Yes?"

"An outside call for you, Lord Holt. Lord McDermott is calling," the bland metallic voice said.

"Lord McDermott's secretary, you mean?"

"It is Lord McDermott himself, your lordship."

Holt blinked. "You're joking," he said. "It's fifty years

since he called me. If this is a prank I'll have your circuits shorted!"

"I cannot joke, your lordship. Shall I tell Lord McDermott you do not wish to speak to him?"

"Of course!" Holt snapped. "No—wait. Find out what he wants. *Then* tell him I can't speak to him."

Holt sank back into a chair in front of the screen. He nudged a button with his elbow, and tiny fingers began to massage the muscles of his back, where the tension poisons had suddenly flooded in to stiffen him.

McDermott calling? What for?

To complain, of course. Some trespass, no doubt. Some serious trespass, if McDermott felt he had to make the call himself.

Michael Holt's blood warmed. Let him complain! Let him accuse, let him bluster! Perhaps this would give the excuse for hostilities at last. Holt ached to declare war. He had been building his armaments patiently for decade after decade, and he knew beyond doubt that he had the capability to destroy McDermott within moments after the first shot was fired. No screens in the universe could withstand the array of weaponry Holt had assembled. The outcome was in no doubt. *Let him start something,* Michael Holt prayed. *Oh, let him be the aggressor! I'm ready for him, and more than ready!*

The bell chimed again. The robot voice of Holt's secretary said, "I have spoken to him, your lordship. He will tell me nothing. He wants you."

Holt sighed. "Very well. Put him on, then."

There was a moment of electronic chaos on the screen as the robot shifted from the inside channel to an outside one. Holt sat stiffly, annoyed by the sudden anxiety he felt. He realized, strangely, that he had forgotten what his enemy's voice sounded like. All communication between them had been through robot intermediaries for years.

The screen brightened and showed a test pattern. A hoarse, querulous voice said, "Holt? Holt, where are you?"

"Right here in my chair, McDermott. What's troubling you?"

"Turn your visual on. Let me have a look at you, Holt."

"You can speak your piece without seeing me, can't you? Is my face that fascinating to you?"

"Please. This is no time for bickering. Turn the visual on!"

"Let me remind you," Holt said coldly, "that *you* have called *me*. The normal rules of etiquette require that I have the privilege of deciding on the manner of transmission. And I prefer not to be seen. I also prefer not to be speaking to you. You have thirty seconds to state your complaint. Important business awaits me."

There was silence. Holt gripped the arms of his chair and signaled for a more intense massage. He became aware, in great irritation, that his hands were trembling. He glared at the screen as though he could burn his enemy's brain out simply by sending angry thoughts over the communicator.

McDermott said finally, "I have no complaint, Holt. Only an invitation."

"To tea?" Holt sneered.

"Call it that. I want you to come here, Holt."

"You've lost your mind!"

"Not yet. Come to me. Let's have a truce," McDermott rasped. "We're both old, sick, stupid men. It's time to stop the hatred."

Holt laughed. "We're both old, yes. But I'm not sick

and you're the only stupid one. Isn't it a little late for the olive branch?"

"Never too late."

"You know there can't ever be peace between us," Holt said. "Not so long as that eyesore of yours sticks up over the trees. It's a cinder in my eye, McDermott. I can't ever forgive you for building it."

"Will you listen to me?" McDermott said. "When I'm gone, you can blast the place apart, if it pleases you. All I want is for you to come here. I—I need you, Holt. I want you to pay me a visit."

"Why don't you come here, then?" Holt jeered. "I'll throw my door wide for you. We'll sit by the fire and reminisce about all the years we hated each other."

"If I could come to you," McDermott said, "there would be no need for us to meet at all."

"What do you mean?"

"Turn your visual on, and you'll see."

Michael Holt frowned. He knew he had become hideous with age, and he was not eager to show himself to his enemy. But he could not see McDermott without revealing himself at the same time. With an abrupt, impulsive gesture, Holt jabbed the control button on his chair. The mists on the screen faded, and an image appeared.

All Holt could see was a face, shrunken, wizened, wasted. McDermott was past two hundred, Holt knew, and he looked it. There was no flesh left on his face. The skin lay like parchment over bone. The left side of his face was distorted, the nostril flared, the mouth-corner dragged down to reveal the teeth, the eyelid drooped. Below the chin, McDermott was invisible, swathed in machinery, his body cocooned in what was probably a nutrient bath. He was obviously in bad shape.

He said, "I've had a stroke, Holt. I'm paralyzed from the neck down. I can't hurt you."

"When did this happen?"

"A year ago."

"You've kept very quiet about it," Holt said.

"I didn't think you'd care to know. But now I do. I'm dying, Holt, and I want to see you once face to face before I die. I know you're suspicious. You think I'm crazy to ask you to come here. I'll turn my screens off. I'll send all my robots across the river. I'll be absolutely alone here, helpless, and you can come with an army if you like. There. Doesn't that sound like a trap, Holt? I know I'd think so if I were in your place and you were in mine. But it isn't a trap. Can you believe that? I'll open my door to you. You can come and laugh in my face as I lie here. But come. There's something I have to tell you, something of vital importance to you. And you've got to be here in person when I tell you. You won't regret coming. Believe that, Holt."

Holt stared at the wizened creature in the screen, and trembled with doubt and confusion.

The man must be a lunatic! It was years since Holt had last stepped beyond the protection of his own screens. Now McDermott was asking him not only to go into the open field, where he might be gunned down with ease, but to enter into McDermott's house itself, to put his head right between the jaws of the lion.

Absurd!

McDermott said, "Let me show you my sincerity. My screens are off. Take a shot at the house. Hit it anywhere. Do your worst!"

Deeply troubled, chilled with mystification, Holt elbowed out of his chair and went beyond the range of the visual pickup, over to the control console of the guns. How many times in dreams had he fondled these studs and knobs, never once daring to fire them except in test shots directed at his own property! It was unreal to be actually training the sights on the gleaming tower of McDermott's house at last. Excitement surged in him. Could this all be some subtle way, he wondered, of causing him to have a fatal heart attack through overstimulation?

He gripped the controls. He pondered, considered tossing a thousand megawatt beam at McDermott, then decided to use something a little milder. If the screens were down all the way, even his feeblest shot would score.

He sighted—not on the house itself, but on a tree just within McDermott's inner circle of defense. He fired, still half convinced he was dreaming. The tree became a yard-high stump.

"That's it," McDermott called. "Go on. Aim at the house, too! Knock a turret off—the screens are down!"

Senile dementia, Holt thought. Baffled, he lifted the sight a bit and let the beam play against one of McDermott's outbuildings. The shielded wall glowed a moment, then gave as the beam smashed its way through. Ten square feet of McDermott's castle now was a soup of protons, fleeing into the cold.

Holt realized in stunned disbelief that there was nothing at all preventing him from destroying McDermott and his odious house entirely.

There was no risk of a counterattack. He would not even need to use the heavy artillery that he had been so jealousy hoarding against this day. A light beam would do it easily enough.

It would be too easy this way, though.

There could be no pleasure in a wanton attack.

McDermott had not provoked him. Rather, he sat there in his cocoon, sniveling and begging to be visited.

Holt returned to the visual field. "I must be as crazy as you are," he said. "Turn your robots loose and leave your screens down. I'll come visit you. I wish I understood this, but I'll come anyway."

III

Michael Holt called his family together. Three wives, the eldest near his own age, the youngest only seventy. Seven sons, ranging in age from sixty to a hundred thirteen. The wives of his sons. His grandchildren. His top echelon of robots.

He assembled them in the grand hall of Holt Keep, took his place at the head of the table, and stared down the rows at their faces, so like his own. He said quietly, "I am going to pay a call on Lord McDermott."

He could see the shock on their faces. They were too well disciplined to speak their minds, of course. He was Lord Holt. His word was law, and he could, if he so pleased, order them all put to death on the spot. Once, many years before, he had been forced to assert his parental authority in just such a way, and no one would ever forget it.

He smiled. "You think I've gone soft in my old age, and perhaps I have. But McDermott has had a stroke. He's completely paralyzed from the neck down. He wants to tell me something, and I'm going to go. His screens are down and he's sending all his robots out of the house. I could have blasted the place apart if I wanted to."

He could see the muscles working in the jaws of his sons. They wanted to cry out, but they did not dare.

Holt went on, "I'm going alone except for a few robots. If there's been no word from me for half an hour after I'm seen entering the house, you're authorized to come after me. If there's any interference with the rescue party, it will mean war. But I don't think there'll be trouble. Anyone who comes after me in less than half an hour will be put to death."

Holt's words died away in a shiver of echoes. He eyed them all, one at a time.

This was a critical moment, he knew. If they dared, they might decide among themselves that he had gone mad, and depose him. That had happened before, too, in other families. They could topple him, reprogram all the robots to take commands from them instead, and confine him to his wing of the house. He had given them evidence enough, just now, of his irresponsibility.

But they made no move. They lacked the guts. He was head of the household, and his word was law. They sat, pale and shaken and dazed, as he rolled his chair past them and out of the grand hall.

Within an hour, he was ready to go. Winter was in the fourth of its seven months, and Michael Holt had not left the house since the first snowfall. But he had nothing to fear from the elements. He would not come in contact with the frigid air of the sub-zero plain. He entered his car within his own house, and it glided out past the defense perimeter, a gleaming dark teardrop sliding over the fresh snow. Eight of his robots accompanied him, a good enough army for almost any emergency.

A visual pickup showed him the scene at McDermott Keep. The robots were filing out, an army of black ants clustering around the great gate. He could see them marching eastward, vanishing from sight beyond the house. A robot overhead reported that they were heading for the river by the dozens.

The miles flew past. Black, twisted trees poked through the snow, and Holt's car weaved a way through them. Far below, under many feet of whiteness, lay the fertile fields. In the spring all would be green. The leafy trees would help to shield the view of McDermott Keep, though they could not hide it altogether. In winter, the ugly copper-colored house was totally visible. That made the winters all the more difficult for Holt to endure.

A robot said softly, "We are approaching the border-lands, your lordship."

"Try a test shot to see if his screens are still down."

"Shall I aim for the house?"

"No. A tree."

Holt watched. A thick-boled, stubby tree in McDer-mott's front palisade gleamed a moment, and then was gone.

"The screens are still down," the robot reported.

"All right. Let's cross the border."

He leaned back against the cushion. The car shot forward. They left the bounds of Holt's own estate, now, and entered McDermott's.

There was no warning ping to tell them they were trespassing. McDermott had even turned off the boundary scanners, then. Holt pressed sweaty palms together. More than ever now he felt that he had let himself be drawn into some sort of trap. There was no turning back now. He was across the border, into McDermott's own territory. Better to die boldly, he thought, than to live huddled in a shell.

He had never been this close to McDermott Keep before. When it was being built, McDermott had invited him to inspect it, but Holt had refused. Nor had he been to the house-warming. Alone among the lords of the planet, he had stayed home to sulk. He could hardly even remember when he had last left his own land at all. There were few places to go on this world, with its fifty estates of great size running through the temperate belt. Whenever Holt thirsted for the companionship of any of his fellow lords, which was not often, he could have it easily enough via telescreen. Some of them came to him, now and then.

It was strange that when he finally did stir to pay a call, it should be a call on McDermott.

Drawing near the enemy keep, he found himself reluctantly admitting that it was less close range than it seemed from the windows of Holt Keep. It was a great blocky building, hundreds of yards long, with a tall octagonal tower rising out of its northern end, a metal spike jabbing perhaps five hundred feet high. The reflected afternoon light, bouncing from the snowfield, gave the metal-sheathed building a curiously oily look, not unattractive at this distance.

"We are within the outer defense perimeter," a robot told Holt.

"Keep going."

The robots sounded worried and perturbed, he thought. Of course, they weren't programmed to show much emotional range, but he could detect a note of puzzlement in what they said and how they said it. They couldn't understand this at all. It did not seem to be an invasion of McDermott Keep—that they could have understood. But it was not a friendly visit, either. The robots did not know what to make of this journey.

They were not alone in their confusion at this most unusual situation, Holt thought grimly. He sat back nervously as he and his guardian robots were swiftly carried forward.

IV

When they were a hundred yards from the great gate of McDermott Keep, the doors swung wide. Holt called McDermott and said, "See that those doors stay open all the time I'm here. If they begin to close, there'll be trouble."

McDermott said, "Don't worry. I'm not planning to play any tricks."

Holt's car shot between the gate walls, and he knew that now he was at the enemy's mercy in earnest. His car rolled up to the open carport, and went on through, so that now he was actually within McDermott Keep. His robots followed him through.

"May I close the carport?"

"Keep it open!" Holt said. "I don't mind the cold."

The hood of his car swung back. His robots helped him out. Holt shivered momentarily as the cold outside air, filtering into the carport, touched him. Then he passed through the irising inner door and, flanked by two sturdy robots, walked slowly but doggedly into the keep.

McDermott's voice reached him over a loudspeaker. "I am on the third floor of the tower," he said. "If I had not sent all the robots away, I could have let one of them guide you."

"You could send a member of your family down," Holt said sourly.

McDermott ignored that. "Continue down the corridor until it turns. Go past the armor room. You will reach a dropshaft that leads upward."

Holt and his robots moved through the silent halls.

The place was like a museum. The dark, high-vaulted corridor was lined with statuary and artifacts, everything musty-looking and depressing. How could anyone want to live in a tomb like this? Holt passed a shadowy room where ancient suits of armor stood mounted. He could not help but compute the cost of shipping such useless things across the light-years from Earth.

They came to the dropshaft. Holt and his two robots entered. A robot nudged the reversing stud, and up they went, into the tower Holt had hated so long. McDermott guided them with a word or two.

They passed down a long hall whose dull, dark walls were set off by a gleaming floor that looked like onyx. A sphincter opened, admitting them to an oval room ringed by windows, exhaling a dry, foul stench of death and decay.

Andrew McDermott sat squarely in the middle of the room, nesting in his life-capsule. A tangled network of tubes and pipes surrounded him. All of McDermott that was visible was a pair of eyes, two shining coals in the wasted face.

"I'm glad you came," McDermott said. His voice, without benefit of electronic amplification, was thin and feeble, like the sound of feathers brushing through the air.

Holt stared at him in fascination. "I never thought I'd see this room," he said.

"I never thought you would, either. But it was good of you to come, Holt. You look well, you know. For a man of your age." The thin lips curled in a grotesque twisted smile. "Of course, you're still a youngster. Not even two hundred yet. I've got you by thirty-odd years."

Holt did not feel like listening to the older man's ramblings. "What is it you wanted?" he asked without warmth. "I'm here, but I'm not going to stay all day. You said you had something vital to tell me."

"Not really to tell," McDermott said. "More to ask. A favor. I want you to kill me, Holt."

"What?"

"It's very simple. Disconnect my feed line. There it is, right by my feet. Just rip it out. I'll be dead in an hour. Or do it even more quickly. Turn off my lungs. This switch, right here. That would be the humane way."

"You have a strange sense of humor," Holt said.

"Do you think so? Top the joke, then. Throw the switch and cap the jest."

"You made me come all the way here to *kill* you?"

"Yes," McDermott said. The blazing eyes were unblinking now. "I've been immobilized for a year now. I'm a vegetable in this thing. I sit here day after day, idle, bored. And healthy. I might live another hundred years—do you realize that, Holt? I've had a stroke, yes. I'm paralyzed. But my body's still vigorous. This damned capsule of mine keeps me in tone. It feeds me and exercises me and— *do you think I want to go on living this way, Holt? Would you?"*

Holt shrugged. "If you want to die, you could ask someone in your family to unplug you."

"I have no family."

"Is that true? You had five sons—"

"Four dead, Holt. The other one gone to Earth. No one lives here any more. I've outlasted them all. I'm as eternal as the heavens. Two hundred thirty years, that's long enough to live. My wives are dead, my grandchildren gone away. They'll come home when they find they've inherited. Not before. There's no one here to throw the switch."

"Your robots," Holt suggested.

Again the grim smile. "You must have special robots, Holt. I don't have any that can be tricked into killing their master. I've tried it. They know what'll happen if my life-capsule is disconnected. They won't do it. *You* do it, Holt! Turn me off. Blow the tower to hell, if it bothers you. You've won the game. The prize is yours."

There was a dryness in Holt's throat, a band of pressure across his chest. He tottered a little.

His robots, ever sensitive to his condition, steadied him and guided him to a chair. He had been on his feet a long time for a man of his age. He sat quietly until the spasm passed.

Then he said, "I won't do it."

"Why not?"

"It's too simple, McDermott. I've hated you too long. I can't just flip a switch and turn you off."

"Bombard me, then. Blast the tower down!"

"Without provocation? Do you think I'm a criminal?" Holt asked.

"What do you want me to do?" McDermott said tiredly. "Order my robots to trespass? Set fire to your orchards? What will provoke you, Holt?"

"Nothing," Holt said. "I don't want to kill you. Get someone else to do it."

The eyes glittered. "You devil," McDermott said. "You absolute devil. I never realized how much you hated me. I send for you in a time of need, asking to be put out of my misery, and will you grant me that? Oh, no. Suddenly you get noble. You won't kill me! You devil, I see right through you. You'll go back to your keep and gloat because I'm a living dead man here. You'll chuckle to yourself because I'm alone and frozen into this capsule. Oh, Holt, it's not right to hate so deeply! I admit I've given offense. I deliberately built the tower here to wound your pride. Punish me, then. Take my life. Destroy my tower. Don't leave me here!"

Holt was silent. He moistened his lips, filled his lungs with breath, got to his feet. He stood straight and tall, towering over the capsule that held his enemy.

"Throw the switch," McDermott begged.

"I'm sorry."

"Devil!"

Holt looked at his robots. "It's time to go," he said. "There's no need for you to guide us. We can find our way out."

V

The teardrop-shaped car sped across the shining snow. Holt said nothing as he made the return journey.

His mind clung to the image of the immobilized McDermott, and there was no room for any other thought. That stench of decay that tingled in his nostrils—that glint of madness in the eyes as they begged for oblivion.

They were crossing the borderlands now. Holt's car broke the warning barrier and got a pinging signal to halt and identify. A robot gave the password, and they went on toward Holt Keep.

His family clustered near the entrance, pale, mystified. Holt walked in under his own steam. They were bursting with questions, but no one dared ask anything. It remained for Holt to say the first word.

He said, "McDermott's a sick, crazy, old man. His family is dead or gone. He's a pathetic and disgusting sight. I don't want to talk about the visit."

Sweeping past them, Holt ascended the shaft to the

command room. He peered out, over the snowy field. There was a double track in the snow, leading to and from McDermott Keep, and the sunlight blazed in the track.

The building shuddered suddenly. Holt heard a hiss and a whine. He flipped on his communicator and a robot voice said, "McDermott Keep is attacking, your lordship. We've deflected a high-energy bombardment."

"Did the screens have any trouble with it?"

"No, your lordship. Not at all. Shall I prepare for a counterattack?"

Holt smiled. "No," he said. "Take defensive measures only. Extend the screens right to the border and keep them there. Don't let McDermott do any harm. He's only trying to provoke me. But he won't succeed."

The tall, gaunt man walked to the control panel. His gnarled hands rested lovingly on the equipment. So they had come to warfare at last, he thought. The cannon of McDermott Keep were doing their puny worst. Flickering needles told the story: whatever McDermott was throwing was being absorbed easily. He didn't have the firepower to do any real harm.

Holt's hands tightened on the controls. Now, he thought, he could blast McDermott Keep to ash. But he would not do it, any more than he would have thrown the switch that would have ended Andrew McDermott's life.

McDermott did not understand. Not cruelty, but simple selfishness, had kept him from killing the enemy lord. Just as, all these years, Holt had refrained from launching an attack he was certain to win. He felt remotely sorry for the paralyzed man locked in the life-capsule. But it was inconceivable that Holt would kill him.

Once you are gone, Andrew, who will I have to hate?

That was the reason he had not killed. For no other reason.

Michael Holt peered through the foot-thick safety glass of his command room window. He saw the zone of brown earth, the snowfield with its fresh track, and the coppery ugliness of McDermott Keep. His intestines writhed at the hideousness of the baroque tower against the horizon. He imagined the skyline as it had looked a hundred years ago, before McDermott had built his foul keep.

He fondled the controls of his artillery bank as though they were a young girl's breasts. Then he turned, slowly and stiffly, making his way across the command room to his chair, and sat quietly, listening to the sound of Andrew McDermott's futile bombardment expending itself against the outer defenses of Holt Keep as the winter night fell.

Halfway House

‥‥━◉━━‥‥

AFTERWARD, AFIERI REALIZED that you must give a life to gain a life. Now, he was too interested simply in staying alive to think much about profundities.

He was *l'uomo dal fuoco in bocca*, the man with fire in his mouth. Cancer clawed at his throat. The vocoder gave him speech; but the raging fire soon would burn through to the core of him, and there would be no more Franco Alfieri. That was hard to accept. So he came to the Fold for aid.

He had the money. That was what it took, in part, to enter that gateway of worlds: money, plenty of it. Those who ran the Fold did not do it for sweet charity's sake. The power drain alone was three million kilowatts every time the Fold was opened. You could power a good-sized city on a load like that. But Alfieri was willing to pay what it cost. The money would shortly be of no use to him whatever, unless the beings on the far side of the Fold gave his life back to him.

"You stand on that bedplate," a technician told him. "Put your feet along the red triangular areas. Grasp the rail—*so*. Then wait."

Alfieri obeyed. He was no longer in the habit of taking such brusque orders, but he forgave the man for his rudeness. To the technician, Alfieri was so much wealthy meat, already going maggotty. Alfieri positioned his feet and looked down at the mirror-bright polish of his pointed black shoes. He grasped the furry yellow skin of the rail. He waited for the power surge.

He knew what would happen. Alfieri had been an engineer in Milan, twenty years back, when the European power grid was just coming in. He understood the workings of the Fold as well as—well, as well as anyone else who was not a mathematician. Alfieri had left engineering to found an industrial empire that sprawled from the Alps to the blue Mediterranean, but he had kept up with technology. He was proud of that. He could walk into any factory, go straight to a workbench, display a rare knowledge of any man's labor. Unlike most top executives, his knowledge was deep as well as broad.

Alfieri knew, then, that when the power surge came, it would momentarily create a condition they called a singularity, found in the natural universe only in the immediate vicinity of stars that were in their last moments of life. A collapsing star, a spent supernova, generates about itself a warp in the universe, a funnel to nowhere, the singularity. As the star shrinks, it approaches its Schwarzchild radius, the critical point when the singularity will devour it. Time runs more slowly for the dying star, as it nears the radius; its faint light shifts conspicuously toward the red; time rushes to infinity as the star is caught and swallowed by the singularity. And a man who happens to be present? He passes into the singularity also. Tidal gravitational forces of infinite strength seize him; he is stretched to the limit and simultaneously compressed, attaining zero volume and infinite density, and he is hurled—somewhere.

They had no dying stars in this laboratory. But for a price they could simulate one. For Alfieri's bundle of *lire* they would strain the universe and create a tiny opening and hurl him through the Fold, to a place where pleated universes met, to a place where incurable diseases were not necessarily incurable.

Alfieri waited, a trim, dapper man of fifty, with thinning sandy hair slicked crosswise over the tanned dome of his skull. He wore the tweed suit he had bought in London in '95, and a matching gray-green tie and his small sapphire ring. He gripped the railing. He was not aware of it when the surge came, and the universe was broken open, and Franco Alfieri was catapulted through a yawning vortex into a place never dreamed of in Newton's philosophy.

The being called Vuor said, "This is Halfway House."

Alfieri looked about him. Superficially, his surroundings had not changed at all. He still stood on a glossy copper bedplate, still grasped a furry rail. The quartz walls of the chamber looked the same. But an alien being now peered in, and Alfieri knew he had been translated through the Fold.

The alien's face was virtually a blank: a slit of a mouth below, slits of eyes above, no visible nostrils, a flat greenish façade, altogether, sitting on a squat neck, a triangular shoulderless trunk, ropy limbs. Alfieri had become accustomed to aliens in his dealings, and the sight of Vuor did not disturb him, though he had never seen one of this sort before.

Alfieri felt sweat churning through his pores. Tongues of flame licked at his throat. He had refused full sedation, for unless Alfieri's mind could work properly he would not be Alfieri. But the pain was terrible.

He said, "How soon can I get help?"

"What is the trouble?"

"Cancer of the throat. You hear my voice? Artificial. The larynx is gone already. There's a malignant beast eating me. Cut it out of me."

The eyeslits closed momentarily. Tentacles twined themselves together in a gesture that might have been sympathy, contempt, or refusal. Vuor's reedy, rasping voice said in passable Italian, "We do not help you here, you understand. This is merely Halfway House, the screening point. We distribute you onward."

"I know. I know. Well, send me to a world where they can cure cancer. I don't have much time left. I'm suffering, and I'm not ready to go. There's still work for me to do on Earth. *Capisce?*"

"What do you do, Franco Alfieri?"

"Didn't my dossier arrive?"

"It did. Tell me about yourself."

Alfieri shrugged. His palms were growing clammy, and he let go of the rail, wishing the alien would let him sit down. "I run an engineering company," he said. "Actually a holding company. Alfieri S.A. We do everything: power distribution, pollution control, robotics. We're getting into planetary transformation. Our operating divisions employ hundreds of thousands of men. We're more than just a money-making concern, though. We're shapers of a better world. We—" He hesitated, realizing that he sounded now like one of his own public relations flunkies and realizing also that he was begging for his own life. "It's a big, important, useful company. I founded it. I run it."

"And you are very rich. For this you wish us to prolong your life? You know that we all live under a sentence of death. For some sooner, others later. The surgeons beyond the Fold cannot save everyone. The number of sufferers who cry out is infinite, Alfieri. Tell me why you should be saved."

Wrath flamed in Alfieri. He suppressed it.

He said, "I'm a human being with a wife and children. Not good enough reason, eh? I'm wealthy enough to pay any price to be healed. Good? No? Of course not. All right, try this: I'm a genius. Like Leonardo, like Michelangelo, like—like Einstein. You know those names? Good. I have a big genius, too. I don't paint, I don't compose music. I plan. I organize. I built the biggest corporation in Europe. I took companies and put them together to do things they could never have done alone."

He glowered at the alien green mask beyond the quartz wall. "The technology that led Earth to open the Fold in the first place—my company. The power source—mine. I built it. I don't boast, I speak the truth."

"You are saying that you have made a lot of money."

"Damn you, no! I'm saying that I've created something that didn't exist before, something useful, something important, not only to Earth but to all the other worlds that meet here. And I'm not through creating. I've got bigger ideas. I need ten more years, and I don't have ten months.

Can you take the responsibility of shutting me off? Can you afford to throw away all that's still in me? Can you?"

His unreal voice, which never grew hoarse even when he raised it to a shout, died away. Alfieri leaned on the railing again. The small golden eyes in the narrow slits regarded him impassively.

After a long silence Vuor said, "We will give you our decision shortly."

The walls of the chamber went opaque. Alfieri paced the little room wearily. The taste of defeat was sour in his mouth, and somehow it did not anger him to know that he had failed. He was past caring. They would let him die, of course. They would tell him that he had done his work, that he had built his company, that it saddened them but they had to consider the needs of younger men whose life-dreams still were unrealized. Then, too, they were likely to think that merely because he was rich he was not deserving of rescue. Easier was it for a camel to go through the eye of a needle, than for a rich man to attain new life on the surgeon's tables of a world beyond the Fold. Yet he couldn't give up now.

As he awaited his death sentence, Alfieri planned how he would spend his remaining months of life. Working to the end, of course. The heatsink project at Spitzbergen— yes, that first, and then—

The walls were clear again. Vuor had returned.

"Alfieri, we have made an appointment for you on Hinnerang, where your cancer will be remitted and your tissues restored. But there is a price."

"Anything. A trillion *lire!*"

"Not money," Vuor said. "Service. Put your genius to work in our aid."

"Tell me how!"

"Halfway House, you know, is cooperatively staffed by representatives of many worlds whose continua meet at the Fold. There is not currently an administrator from Earth on our staff. A vacancy is soon to develop. You fill it. Lend us your gift for organizing, for administration. Take a five-year term among us. Then you may return home."

Alfieri pondered. He had no particular wish to give up five years to this place. Too much beckoned to him on Earth, and if he were away five years, who would take the reins of his companies? He might return and find himself hopelessly out of touch.

Then he realized the absurdity of the thought. Vuor was offering him twenty, thirty, fifty more years of life. Standing at the edge of the grave as he was, Alfieri had no right to begrudge five of those years if his benefactors demanded them. He had made his unique administrative abilities his claim for renewed life; was it any surprise that they now wanted those same abilities as *quid pro quo*?

"Agreed," Alfieri said.

"There will, in addition, be a monetary payment," said Vuor, but Alfieri hardly cared about that.

An infinity of universes met at the Fold, as they did at every other point in space–time. Only at the Fold, though, was it possible now to cross from one continuum to another, thanks to the equipment installed there. A webwork of singularities poked holes in the fabric of universal structures. Halfway House was the shuttle point for this loom of worlds; those who could convince the administrators that they had the right to occupy a valuable place on the transfer channels were shunted to the worlds of their need.

An infinity is an infinity, and the channels filled all needs. There was access, for those who wanted it, to a matter-free universe and to a universe filled with one all-encompassing atom and to a universe containing a world where living beings grew steadily younger and not the reverse.

There were worlds unknown to the sons of Adam, with tribes whose heads grow beneath their shoulders and their mouths in their breasts; worlds of monoculi, who run swiftly though they have a single leg and a single eye; worlds of folk whose mouths are so small they take nourishment only through a straw; worlds of amoebic intelligences; worlds where bodily reincarnation is an established fact; worlds where dreams become realities at the snap of a finger. An infinity is an infinity. But for practical purposes, only some two dozen of these worlds mattered, for they were the ones linked by common purposes and common orientation.

On one of those worlds, skilled surgeons might repair a cancer-ravaged throat. In time that skill would be imparted to Earth in return for some Earthly good, but Alfieri could not wait for the exchange to be consummated. He paid his fee, and the administrators of Halfway House sent him to Hinnerang.

Alfieri was unaware, once again, as he squeezed through the Schwarzchild singularity. He had always loved tasting unfamiliar sensations, and it seemed unfair to him that a man should be compressed to zero volume and infinite density without some tactile knowledge of the fact. But so it happened. A dying supernova was simulated for him, and he was whisked through the singularity to emerge in one more identical chamber on Hinnerang.

Here, at least, things looked properly alien. There was

a reddish tinge to the warm, golden sunlight, and at night four moons danced in the sky. The gravity was half that of Earth's; and as he stood under that quartet of shimmering orbs, Alfieri felt a strange giddiness and an inner access of ecstatic strength. It seemed to him that he could leap at a bound and snatch one of those jewels from the sky.

The Hinnerangi were small, angular beings with auburn skins, high-vaulted skullcaps, and fibrous fingers that divided and divided again until they formed writhing networks of filament at the tips. They spoke in sinister whispers, and their language struck Alfieri as more barbarous than Basque and as consonant-heavy as Polish; but the usual small devices turned their words to the tongue of Dante when they needed to communicate with him, a miracle that struck Alfieri as more awesome than the whole mechanism of the Fold, which at least he could pretend he understood.

"We will first negate your pain," his surgeon told him.

"By knocking out my pain sensors?" Alfieri asked. "Cutting nerve lines?"

The surgeon regarded him with what seemed like grave amusement. "There are no pain sensors as such in the human nervous system. There are merely functional bodies that perceive and respond by classifying the many patterns of nerve impulses arriving from the skin, selecting and abstracting the necessary modalities. 'Pain' is simply a label for a class of experiences, not always unpleasant. We will adjust the control center, the gate of responses, so that your scanning of input impulses will be orientated differently. There will be no loss of sensory information; but what you feel will no longer be classified as pain."

At another time, Alfieri might have been happy to discuss the refined semantics of pain theory. Now, he was satisfied to nod solemnly and permit them to put out the fire that raged in his throat.

It was done, delicately and simply. He lay in a cradle of some gummy foam while the surgeon planned the next move: a major resection of tissue; replacement of lost cell matter; regeneration of organs. To Alfieri, wireless transmission of power was an everyday matter, but these things were the stuff of dreams. He submitted. They cut away so much of him that it seemed another slice of the surgical beam would sever his head altogether. Then they rebuilt him. When they were finished, he would speak with his own voice again, not with an implanted mechanism. But would it really be his own, if they had built it for him? No matter. It was flesh. Alfieri's heart pumped Alfieri's blood through the new tissue.

And the cancer? Was it gone?

The Hinnerangi were thorough. They hunted the berserk cells through the corridors of his body. Alfieri saw colonies of cancer establishing themselves in his lungs, his kidneys, his intestines. He visualized marauding creatures stabbing good cells with mortal wounds, thrusting their own vile fluid into unwanted places, replicating a legion of goose-stepping carcinomas cell by cell by cell. But the Hinnerangi were thorough. They purged Alfieri of corruption. They took out his appendix, in the bargain, and comforted his liver against a lifetime of white Milanese wine. Then they sent him off to recuperate.

He breathed alien air and watched moons leaping like gazelles in a sky of strange constellations. He put his hand to his throat a thousand times a day, to feel the newness there, the warmth of fresh tissue. He ate the meat of unknown beasts. He gained strength from hour to hour.

At last they put him in a singularity chamber and rammed him through the complexities of the Fold, and he returned to Halfway House.

Vuor said, "You will begin your work at once. This will be your office."

It was an oval room, walled with a living plastic that made it seem as warm and pink and soft as the walls of a womb. Beyond one wall was the quartz-bounded chamber used by those who traveled the Fold. Vuor showed him how to operate the switch that permitted viewing access to the chamber in either direction.

"What will my duties be?" Alfieri asked.

"Come and tour Halfway House first," said Vuor.

Alfieri followed. It was hard to grasp the nature of the place; Alfieri pictured it as something like a space station, an orbiting wheel of finite size divided into many chambers. But since there were no windows, he could not confirm that belief. The place seemed fairly small, no bigger than a good-sized office building. Much of it was given over to a power plant. Alfieri wished to stay and examine the generators, but Vuor hurried him on to a cafeteria, to a small room that would be his dwelling place, to some sort of chapel, to executive offices.

The alien seemed impatient. Silent figures drifted through the halls of Halfway House, beings of fifty sorts. Nearly all were oxygen breathers who could handle the all-purpose atmosphere of the place, but some were masked and mysterious. They nodded at Vuor, stared at Alfieri. Civil servants, Alfieri thought. Doing their routine work. And now I am one of them, a petty bureaucrat. But I am alive, and I will wade through a sea of bureaucratic forms to show my gratitude.

They returned to the oval office with the soft, moist pink walls.

"What will my duties be?" Alfieri asked again.

"To interview those who come to Halfway House seeking to travel beyond the Fold."

"But that's your job!"

"No longer," said Vuor. "My term is up. Mine is the now-vacant position you have been recruited to fill. When you begin, I can leave."

"You said I'd get an administrative post. To organize, to plan—"

"This is administrative work. You must judge the niceties of each applicant's situation. You must be aware of the capacity of the facilities beyond this point. You must maintain an overview of your task: whom to send forward, whom to reject."

Alfieri's hands trembled. "I'm the one who'll decide? I say, go back and rot, and you come forward? I choose life for some and death for others? No. I don't want it. I'm not God!"

"Neither am I," said the alien blandly. "Do you think I like this job? But now I can shrug it off. I am finished here. I have been God for five years, Alfieri. It's your turn now."

"Give me some other work. There must be other jobs suited for me!"

"Perhaps there are. But you are best suited for this one. You are a gifted decider. And another thing to consider, Alfieri. You are my replacement. If you do not take the job, I must remain until someone else capable of handling it is found. I have been God long enough, Alfieri."

Alfieri was silent. He stared into the golden eyeslits, and for the first time he thought he could interpret an expression he found there. Pain. The pain of an Atlas, carrying worlds on his shoulders. Vuor was suffering. And he,

Franco Alfieri, could alleviate that pain by taking the burden on himself.

Vuor said, "When your application was approved, there was an understanding that you would render service to us. The scope of your duties has been outlined to you. There is an obligation, Alfieri."

Nodding, Alfieri saw the truth of that. If he refused to take the post, what would they do? Give him his cancer back? No. They would find another use for him. And Vuor would continue to hold this job. Alfieri owed his life to the suffering alien. If he extended Vuor's duties by one additional hour, it would be unforgivable.

"I accept the obligation," Alfieri said.

The look in the alien's eyeslits could have been nothing but joy.

There were certain things Alfieri had to learn about his job, and then he was on his own. He learned them. He took up his new existence as a bureaucrat with good grace. One room to live in, instead of a cycle of mansions; food prepared by computers, not by master chefs; a long day of work, and little recreation. But he was alive. He could look to a time beyond the five years.

He sent word to Earth that he would be detained and that he would eventually return in good health to resume his position in the corporation. He authorized the commencement of Plan A for running the company in his prolonged absence. Alfieri had planned everything. Men he trusted would be stewards for him until he returned. It was made quite clear to him at Halfway House that he could not attempt to run the firm by remote control, and so he activated his plan and left the company to its new administrators. He was busy enough.

Applicants came to him.

Not all of them wished medical aid, but all had some good and compelling reason for journeying to some world beyond the Fold. Alfieri judged their cases. He had no quota; if he cared to, he could send all his applicants through to their destinations or turn them all away. But the one would be irresponsible, the other inhumane. Alfieri judged. He weighed in the balance, and some he found wanting, and others he passed on. There were only so many channels, a finite number of routes to the infinity of worlds. Alfieri thought of himself sometimes as a traffic policeman, sometimes as Maxwell's Demon, sometimes as Rhadamanthys in Hades. Mostly he thought of the day when he could go home again.

The refusals were painful. Some of the applicants bellowed their rage at him and made threats. Some of them shrank into sobbing stupors. Some quietly warned of the grave injustice he was doing. Alfieri had made hard decisions all his life, but his soul was not yet calloused from them, and he regretted the things the applicants said to him. The job, though, had to be done, and he could not deny he had a gift for it.

He was not the only such judge at Halfway House, naturally. Streams of applicants were constantly processed through many offices. But Alfieri was, in addition to a judge, the final court of appeals for his colleagues. He maintained the overview. He controlled the general flow. It was his talent to administer things.

A day came when an auburn-skinned being with swarming subdivided tendrils stood before him, a man of Hinnerang. For a terrible moment Alfieri thought it was the surgeon who had repaired his throat. But the resemblance was only superficial. This man was no surgeon.

Alfieri said, "This is Halfway House."

"I need help. I am Tomrik Horiman. You have my dossier?"

"I do," Alfieri said. "You know that we give no help here, Tomrik Horiman. We simply forward you to the place where help may be obtained. Tell me about yourself."

The tendrils writhed in anguish. "I am a grower of houses. My capital is overextended. My entire establishment is threatened. If I could go to a world where my houses would win favor, my firm would be saved. I have a plan for growing houses on Melknor. Our calculations show that there would be a demand for our product there."

"Melknor has no shortage of houses," Alfieri remarked.

"But they love novelty there. They'd rush to buy. An entire family is faced with ruin, kind sir! Root and branch we will be wiped out. The penalty for bankruptcy is extreme. With my honor lost, I would have to destroy myself. I have children."

Alfieri knew that. He also knew that the Hinnerangi spoke the truth; unless he were allowed to pass through to Melknor to save his business, he would be obliged to take his own life. As much as Alfieri himself, this being had come before the tribunal of Halfway House under a death sentence.

But Alfieri had gifts. What did this man offer? He wished to sell houses on a planet that had no real need for them. He was one of many such house-growers, anyway, and a poor businessman to boot. He had brought his troubles upon himself, unlike Alfieri, who had not asked for his cancer. Nor would Tomrik Horiman's passing be any great loss except to his immediate family. It was a great pity; but the application would have to be refused.

"We will give you our decision shortly," said Alfieri. He opaqued the walls and briefly reported to his colleagues. They did not question the wisdom of his decision. Clearing the walls, he stared through the blocks of quartz at the man from Hinnerang and said, "I greatly regret that your application must be rejected."

Alfieri waited for the reaction. Anger? Hysterical denunciation? Despair? Cold fury? A paroxysm of frustration?

No, none of those. The merchant of vegetary houses looked back at Alfieri, who had spent enough time among the Hinnerangi to interpret their unvoiced emotions. And Alfieri felt the flood of sorrow coming at him like a stream of acid. Tomrik Horiman *pitied* him.

"I am very sorry," the Hinnerangi said. "You bear such a great burden."

Alfieri shook with the pain of the words. The man was sorry—not for himself, but for *him*! Morbidly, he almost wished for his cancer back. Tomrik Horiman's pity was more than he could bear at that moment.

Tomrik Horiman gripped the rail and stood poised for his return to his own world. For an instant his eyes met the shadowed ones of the Earthman.

"Tell me," Tomrik Horiman said. "This job you have, deciding who goes forward, who goes back. Such a terrible burden! How did this job come to you?"

"I was condemned to it," said Franco Alfieri in all the anguish of his Godhead. "The price for my life was my life. I never knew such suffering when I was only a dying man."

He scowled. And then he threw the switch that sent Tomrik Horiman away.

Sundance

◄─◉─►

Today you liquidated about 50,000 Eaters in Sector A, and now you are spending an uneasy night. You and Herndon flew east at dawn, with the green-gold sunrise at your backs, and sprayed the neural pellets over a thousand hectares along the Forked River. You flew on into the prairie beyond the river, where the Eaters have already been wiped out, and had lunch sprawled on that thick, soft carpet of grass where the first settlement is expected to rise. Herndon picked some juiceflowers and you enjoyed half an hour of mild hallucinations. Then, as you headed toward the copter to begin an afternoon of further pellet-spraying, he said suddenly, "Tom, how would you feel about this if it turned out that the Eaters weren't just animal pests? That they were *people*, say, with a language and rites and a history and all?"

You thought of how it had been for your own people. "They aren't," you said.

"Suppose they were. Suppose the Eaters—"

"They aren't. Drop it."

Herndon has this streak of cruelty in him that leads him to ask such questions. He goes for the vulnerabilities; it amuses him. All night now his casual remark has echoed in your mind. Suppose the Eaters. . . . Suppose the Eaters. . . . Suppose. . . . Suppose. . . .

You sleep for a while, and dream, and in your dreams you swim through rivers of blood.

Foolishness. A feverish fantasy. You know how important it is to exterminate the Eaters fast, before the settlers get here. They're just animals, and not even harmless animals at that; ecology-wreckers is what they are, devourers of oxygen-liberating plants, and they have to go. A few have been saved for zoological study. The rest must be destroyed. Ritual extirpation of undesirable beings: the old, old story. But let's not complicate our job with moral qualms, you tell yourself. Let's not dream of rivers of blood.

The Eaters don't even *have* blood, none that could flow in rivers, anyway. What they have is, well, a kind of lymph that permeates every tissue and transmits nourishment along the interfaces. Waste products go out the same way, osmotically. In terms of process it's structurally analogous to your own kind of circulatory system, except there's no network of blood vessels hooked to a master pump. The life-stuff just oozes through their bodies, as though they were amoebas or sponges or some other low-phylum form. Yet they're definitely high-phylum in nervous system, digestive set-up, limb-and-organ template, etc.

Odd, you think. The thing about aliens is that they're alien, you tell yourself, not for the first time.

The beauty of their biology for you and your companions is that it lets you exterminate them so neatly.

You fly over the grazing grounds and drop the neural pellets. The Eaters find and ingest them. Within an hour the poison has reached all sectors of the body. Life ceases; a rapid breakdown of cellular matter follows, the Eater literally falling apart molecule by molecule the instant that nutrition is cut off; the lymph-like stuff works like acid; a universal lysis occurs; flesh and even the bones, which are cartilaginous, dissolve. In two hours, a puddle on the ground. In four, nothing at all left. Considering how many millions of Eaters you've scheduled for extermination here, it's sweet of the bodies to be self-disposing. Otherwise what a charnel-house this world would become!

Suppose the Eaters. . . .

Damn Herndon. You almost feel like getting a memory-editing in the morning. Scrape his stupid speculations out of your head. If you dared. If you dared.

In the morning he does not dare. Memory-editing frightens him; he will try to shake free of his newfound guilt without it. The Eaters, he explains to himself, are mindless herbivores, the unfortunate victims of human expansionism, but not really deserving of passionate defense. Their extermination is not tragic; it's just too bad. If Earthmen are to have this world, the Eaters must relinquish it. There's a difference, he tells himself, between the elimination of the Plains Indians from the American prairie in the nineteenth century and the destruction of the bison on that same prairie. One feels a little wistful about the slaughter of the thundering herds; one regrets the butchering of millions of the noble brown woolly beasts, yes. But one feels outrage, not mere wistful regret, at what was done to the Sioux. There's a difference. Reserve your passions for the proper cause.

He walks from his bubble at the edge of the camp toward the center of things. The flagstone path is moist and glistening. The morning fog has not yet lifted, and every tree is bowed, the long notched leaves heavy with droplets of water. He pauses, crouching, to observe a spider-analog spinning its asymmetrical web. As he watches, a small amphibian, delicately shaded turquoise, glides as inconspicuously as possible over the mossy ground. Not inconspicuously enough; he gently lifts the little creature and puts it on the back of his hand. The gills flutter in anguish and the amphibian's sides quiver. Slowly, cunningly, its color changes until it matches the coppery tone of the hand. The camouflage is excellent. He lowers his hand and the amphibian scurries into a puddle. He walks on.

He is forty years old, shorter than most of the other members of the expedition, with wide shoulders, a heavy chest, dark glossy hair, a blunt spreading nose. He is a biologist. This is his third career, for he has failed as an anthropologist and as a developer of real estate. His name is Tom Two Ribbons. He has been married twice but has had no children. His great-grandfather died of alcoholism; his grandfather was addicted to hallucinogens; his father had compulsively visited cheap memory-editing parlors. Tom Two Ribbons is conscious that he is failing a family tradition, but he has not yet found his own mode of self-destruction.

In the main building he discovers Herndon, Julia,

Ellen, Schwartz, Chang, Michaelson, and Nichols. They
are eating breakfast; the others are already at work. Ellen
rises and comes to him and kisses him. Her short soft
yellow hair tickles his cheeks. "I love you," she whispers.
She has spent the night in Michaelson's bubble. "I love
you," he tells her, and draws a quick vertical line of affec-
tion between her small pale breasts. He winks at Michaelson, who nods, touches the tips of two fingers to his lips,
and blows them a kiss. We are all good friends here, Tom
Two Ribbons thinks.

"Who drops pellets today?" he asks.

"Mike and Chang," says Julia. "Sector C."

Schwartz says, "Eleven more days and we ought to
have the whole peninsula clear. Then we can move
inland."

"If our pellet supply holds up," Chang points out.

Herndon says, "Did you sleep well, Tom?"

"No," says Tom. He sits down and taps out his breakfast requisition. In the west the fog is beginning to burn
off the mountains. Something throbs in the back of his
neck. He has been on this world nine weeks, now, and in
that time it has undergone its only change of season,
shading from dry weather to foggy. The mists will remain
for many months. Before the plains parch again the Eaters
will be gone and the settlers will begin to arrive. His food
slides down the chute and he seizes it. Ellen sits beside
him. She is a little more than half his age; this is her first
voyage; she is their keeper of records, but she also is
skilled at editing. "You look troubled," Ellen tells him.
"Can I help you?"

"No. Thank you."

"I hate it when you get gloomy."

"It's a racial trait," says Tom Two Ribbons.

"I doubt that very much."

"The truth is that maybe my personality reconstruct is wearing thin. The trauma level was so close to the surface. I'm just a walking veneer, you know."

Ellen laughs prettily. She wears only a sprayon half-wrap. Her skin looks damp; she and Michaelson have had a swim at dawn. Tom Two Ribbons is thinking of asking her to marry him, when this job is over. He has not been married since the collapse of the real estate business. The therapist suggested divorce as part of the reconstruct. He sometimes wonders where Terry has gone and who she lives with now. Ellen says, "You seem pretty stable to me, Tom."

"Thank you," he says. She is young. She does not know.

"If it's just a passing gloom I can edit it out in one quick snip."

"Thank you," he says. "No."

"I forget. You don't like editing."

"My father—"

"Yes."

"In fifty years he pared himself down to a thread," Tom Two Ribbons says. "He had his ancestors edited away, his whole heritage, his religion, his wife, his sons, finally his name. Then he sat and smiled all day. Thank you, no editing."

"Where are you working today?" Ellen asks.

"In the compound, running tests."

"Want company? I'm off all morning."

"Thank you, no," he says, too quickly. She looks hurt. He tries to remedy his unintended cruelty by touching her arm lightly and saying, "Maybe this afternoon, all right? I need to commune a while. Yes?"

"Yes," she says, and smiles, and shapes a kiss with her lips.

After breakfast he goes to the compound. It covers a thousand hectares east of the base; they have bordered it with neural-field projectors at intervals of eighty meters, and this is a sufficient fence to keep the captive population of two hundred Eaters from straying. When all the others have been exterminated, this study group will remain. At the southwest corner of the compound stands a lab bubble from which the experiments are run: metabolic, psychological, physiological, ecological. A stream crosses the compound diagonally. There is a low ridge of grassy hills at its eastern edge. Five distinct copses of tightly clustered knifeblade trees are separated by patches of dense savanna. Sheltered beneath the grass are the oxygen-plants, almost completely hidden except for the photosynthetic spikes that jut to heights of three or four meters at regular intervals, and for the lemon-colored respiratory bodies, chest-high, that make the grassland sweet and dizzying with exhaled gases. Through the fields move the Eaters in a straggling herd, nibbling delicately at the respiratory bodics. Tom Two Ribbons spies the herd beside the stream and goes toward it. He stumbles over an oxygen-plant hidden in the grass, but deftly recovers his balance and, seizing the puckered orifice of the respiratory body, inhales deeply. His despair lifts. He approaches the Eaters. They are spherical, bulky, slow-moving creatures, covered by masses of coarse orange fur. Saucerlike eyes protrude above narrow rubbery lips; their legs are thin and scaly, like a chicken's, and their arms are short and held close to their bodies. They regard him with bland lack of curiosity. "Good morning, brothers!" is the way he greets them this time and he wonders why.

I noticed something strange today. Perhaps I simply sniffed too much oxygen in the fields; maybe I was succumbing to a suggestion Herndon planted; or possibly it's the family masochism cropping out. But while I was observing the Eaters in the compound it seemed to me, for the first time, that they were behaving intelligently, that they were functioning in a ritualized way.

I followed them around for three hours. During that time they uncovered half a dozen outcroppings of oxygen-plants. In each case they went through a stylized pattern of action before starting to munch. They:

· Formed a straggly circle around the plants.
· Looked toward the sun.
· Looked toward their neighbors on left and right around the circle.
· Made fuzzy neighing sounds *only* after having done the foregoing.
· Looked toward the sun again.
· Moved in and ate.

If this wasn't a prayer of thanksgiving, a saying of grace, then what was it? And if they're advanced enough spiritually to say grace, are we not therefore committing genocide here? Do chimpanzees say grace? Christ, we wouldn't even wipe out chimps the way we're cleaning out the Eaters! Of course, chimps don't interfere with human crops, and some kind of coexistence would be possible, whereas Eaters and human agriculturalists simply can't function on the same planet. Nevertheless there's a moral issue here. The liquidation effort is predicated on the assumption that the intelligence level of the Eaters is about on a par with that of oysters, or, at best, sheep. Our consciences stay clear because our poison is quick and painless and because the Eaters thoughtfully dissolve upon dying, sparing us the mess of incinerating millions of corpses. But if they pray—

I won't say anything to the others just yet. I want more evidence, hard, objective. Films, tapes, record cubes. Then we'll see. What if I can show that we're exterminating intelligent beings? My family knows a little about genocide, after all, having been on the receiving end just a few centuries back. I doubt that I could halt what's going on here. But at the very least I could withdraw from the operation. Head back to Earth and stir up public outcries.

I hope I'm imagining this.

I'm not imagining a thing. They gather in circles; they look to the sun; they neigh and pray. They're only balls of jelly on chicken-legs, but they give thanks for their food. Those big round eyes now seem to stare accusingly at me. Our tame herd here knows what's going on: that we have descended from the stars to eradicate their kind, and that they alone will be spared. They have no way of fighting back or even of communicating their displeasure, but they *know*. And hate us. Jesus, we have killed two million of them since we got here, and in a metaphorical way I'm stained with blood, and what will I do, what can I do?

I must move very carefully, or I'll end up drugged and edited.

I can't let myself seem like a crank, a quack, an agitator. I can't stand up and Denounce. I have to find allies. Herndon, first. He surely is on to the truth; he's the one who nudged *me* to it, that day we dropped pellets. And I thought he was merely being vicious in his usual way!

I'll talk to him tonight.

He says, "I've been thinking about that suggestion you made. About the Eaters. Perhaps we haven't made sufficiently close psychological studies. I mean, if they really *are* intelligent—"

Herndon blinks. He is a tall man with glossy dark hair, a heavy beard, sharp cheekbones. "Who says they are, Tom?"

"You did. On the far side of the Forked River, you said—"

"It was just a speculative hypothesis. To make conversation."

"No, I think it was more than that. You really believed it."

Herndon looks troubled. "Tom, I don't know what you're trying to start, but don't start it. If I for a moment believed we were killing intelligent creatures, I'd run for an editor so fast I'd start an implosion wave."

"Why did you ask me that thing, then?" Tom Two Ribbons says.

"Idle chatter."

"Amusing yourself by kindling guilts in somebody else? You're a bastard, Herndon. I mean it."

"Well, look, Tom, if I had any idea that you'd get so worked up about a hypothetical suggestion—" Herndon shakes his head. "The Eaters aren't intelligent beings. Obviously. Otherwise we wouldn't be under orders to liquidate them."

"Obviously," says Tom Two Ribbons.

Ellen said, "No, I don't know what Tom's up to. But I'm pretty sure he needs a rest. It's only a year and a half since his personality reconstruct, and he had a pretty bad breakdown back then."

Michaelson consulted a chart. "He's refused three times in a row to make his pellet-dropping run. Claiming he can't take time away from his research. Hell, we can fill in for him, but it's the idea that he's ducking chores that bothers me."

"What kind of research is he doing?" Nichols wanted to know.

"Not biological," said Julia. "He's with the Eaters in the compound all the time, but I don't see him making any tests on them. He just watches them."

"And talks to them," Chang observed.

"And talks, yes," Julia said.

"About what?" Nichols asked.

"Who knows?"

Everyone looked at Ellen. "You're closest to him," Michaelson said. "Can't you bring him out of it?"

"I've got to know what he's in, first," Ellen said. "He isn't saying a thing."

You know that you must be very careful, for they out-number you, and their concern for your mental welfare can be deadly. Already they realize you are disturbed, and Ellen has begun to probe for the source of the disturbance. Last night you lay in her arms and she questioned you, obliquely, skillfully, and you knew what she is trying to find out. When the moons appeared she suggested that you and she stroll in the compound, among the sleeping Eaters. You declined; but she sees that you have become involved with the creatures.

You have done probing of your own—subtly, you hope. And you are aware that you can do nothing to save the Eaters. An irrevocable commitment has been made. It is 1876 all over again; these are the bison, these are the

Sioux, and they must be destroyed, for the railroad is on its way. If you speak out here, your friends will calm you and pacify you and edit you, for they do not see what you see. If you return to Earth to agitate, you will be mocked and recommended for another reconstruct. You can do nothing. You can do nothing.

You cannot save, but perhaps you can record.

Go out into the prairie. Live with the Eaters; make yourself their friend; learn their ways. Set it down, a full account of their culture, so that at least that much will not be lost. You know the techniques of field anthropology. As was done for your people in the old days, do now for the Eaters.

He finds Michaelson. "Can you spare me for a few weeks?" he asks.

"Spare you, Tom? What do you mean?"

"I've got some field studies to do. I'd like to leave the base and work with Eaters in the wild."

"What's wrong with the ones in the compound?"

"It's the last chance with wild ones, Mike. I've got to go."

"Alone, or with Ellen?"

"Alone."

Michaelson nods slowly. "All right, Tom. Whatever you want. Go. I won't hold you here."

I dance in the prairie under the green-gold sun. About me the Eaters gather. I am stripped; sweat makes my skin glisten; my heart pounds. I talk to them with my feet, and they understand.

They understand.

They have a language of soft sounds. They have a god.

They know love and awe and rapture. They have rites. They have names. They have a history. Of all this I am convinced.

I dance on thick grass.

How can I reach them? With my feet, with my hands, with my grunts, with my sweat. They gather by the hundreds, by the thousands, and I dance. I must not stop. They cluster about me and make their sounds. I am a conduit for strange forces. My great-grandfather should see me now! Sitting on his porch in Wyoming, the firewater in his hand, his brain rotting—see me now, old one! See the dance of Tom Two Ribbons! I talk to these strange ones with my feet under a sun that is the wrong color. I dance. I dance.

"Listen to me," I say. "I am your friend, I alone, the only one you can trust. Trust me, talk to me, teach me. Let me preserve your ways, for soon the destruction will come."

I dance, and the sun climbs, and the Eaters murmur.

There is the chief. I dance toward him, back, toward, I bow, I point to the sun, I imagine the being that lives in that ball of flame, I imitate the sounds of these people, I kneel, I rise, I dance. Tom Two Ribbons dances for you.

I summon skills my ancestors forgot. I feel the power flowing in me. As they danced in the days of the bison, I dance now, beyond the Forked River.

I dance, and now the Eaters dance, too. Slowly, uncertainly, they move toward me, they shift their weight, lift leg and leg, sway about. "Yes, like that!" I cry. "Dance!"

We dance together as the sun reaches noon height.

Now their eyes are no longer accusing. I see warmth and kinship. I am their brother, their redskinned tribesman, he who dances with them. No longer do they seem clumsy to me. There is a strange ponderous grace in their movements. They dance. They dance. They caper about me. Closer, closer, closer!

We move in holy frenzy.

They sing, now, a blurred hymn of joy. They throw forth their arms, unclench their little claws. In unison they shift weight, left foot forward, right, left, right. Dance, brothers, dance, dance, dance! They press against me. Their flesh quivers; their smell is a sweet one. They gently thrust me across the field, to a part of the meadow where the grass is deep and untrampled. Still dancing, we seek for the oxygen-plants, and find clumps of them beneath the grass, and they make their prayer and seize them with their awkward arms, separating the respiratory bodies from the photosynthetic spikes. The plants, in anguish, release floods of oxygen. My mind reels. I laugh and sing. The Eaters are nibbling the lemon-colored perforated globes, nibbling the stalks as well. They thrust their plants at me. It is a religious ceremony, I see. Take from us, eat with us, join with us, this is the body, this is the blood, take, eat, join. I bend forward and put a lemon-colored globe to my lips. I do not bite; I nibble, as they do, my teeth slicing away the skin of the globe. Juice spurts into my mouth, while oxygen drenches my nostrils. The Eaters sing hosannahs. I should be in full paint for this, paint of my forefathers, feathers too, meeting their religion in the regalia of what should have been mine. Take, eat, join. The juice of the oxygen-plant flows in my veins. I embrace my brothers. I sing, and as my voice leaves my lips it becomes an arch that glistens like new steel, and I pitch my song lower, and the arch turns to tarnished silver. The Eaters crowd close. The scent of their bodies is fiery red to me. Their soft cries are puffs of steam. The sun is very warm; its rays are tiny jagged pings of puckered sound, close to the top of my range of hearing, plink! plink! plink! The thick grass hums to me, deep and rich, and the wind hurls points of flame along the prairie. I devour another oxygen-plant, and then a third. My brothers laugh and shout. They tell me of their gods, the god of warmth, the god of food, the god of pleasure, the god of death, the god of holiness, the god of wrongness, and the others. They recite for me the names of their kings, and I hear their voices as splashes of green mold on the clean sheet of the sky. They instruct me in their holy rites. I must remember this, I tell myself, for when it is gone it will never come again. I continue to dance. They continue to dance. The color of the hills becomes rough and coarse, like abrasive gas. Take, eat, join. Dance. They are so gentle!

I hear the drone of the copter, suddenly.

It hovers far overhead. I am unable to see who flies in it. "No," I scream. "Not here! Not these people! Listen to me! This is Tom Two Ribbons! Can't you hear me? I'm doing a field study here! You have no right—!"

My voice makes spirals of blue moss edged with red sparks. They drift upward and are scattered by the breeze.

I yell, I shout, I bellow. I dance and shake my fists. From the wings of the copter the jointed arms of the pellet-distributors unfold. The gleaming spigots extend and whirl. The neural pellets rain down into the meadow, each tracing a blazing track that lingers in the sky. The sound of the copter becomes a furry carpet stretching to the horizon, and my shrill voice is lost in it.

The Eaters drift away from me, seeking the pellets, scratching at the roots of the grass to find them. Still dancing, I leap into their midst, striking the pellets from their hands, hurling them into the stream, crushing them to powder. The Eaters growl black needles at me. They turn away and search for more pellets. The copter turns and flies off, leaving a trail of dense oily sound. My brothers are gobbling the pellets in terrible eagerness.

There is no way to prevent it.

Joy consumes them and they topple and lie still. Occasionally a limb twitches; then even this stops. They begin to dissolve. Thousands of them melt on the prairie, sinking into shaplessness, losing their spherical forms, flattening, ebbing into the ground. The bonds of the molecules will no longer hold. It is the twilight of protoplasm. They perish. They vanish. For hours I walk the prairie. Now I inhale oxygen; now I eat a lemon-colored globe. Sunset begins with the ringing of leaden chimes. Black clouds make brazen trumpet-calls in the east and the deepening wind is a swirl of coaly bristles. Silence comes. Night falls. I dance. I am alone.

The copter comes again, and they find you, and you do not resist as they gather you in. You are beyond bitterness. Quietly you explain what you have done and what you have learned, and why it is wrong to exterminate these people. You describe the plant you have eaten and the way it affects your senses, and as you talk of the blessed synesthesia, the texture of the wind and the sound of the clouds and the timbre of the sunlight, they nod and smile and tell you not to worry, that everything will be all right soon, and they touch something cold to your forearm, so cold that it is almost into the ultraviolet where you cannot see it, and there is a whir and a buzz and the deintoxicant sinks into your vein and soon the ecstasy drains away, leaving only the exhaustion and the grief.

He says, "We never learn a thing, do we? We export all our horrors to the stars. Wipe out the Armenians, wipe out the Jews, wipe out the Tasmanians, wipe out the Indians, wipe out everyone who's in the way, and then come out here and do the same damned murderous thing. You weren't with me out there. You didn't dance with them. You didn't see what a rich, complex culture the Eaters have. Let me tell you about their tribal structure. It's dense: seven levels of matrimonial relationships, to begin with, and an exogamy factor that requires—"

Softly Ellen says, "Tom, darling, nobody's going to harm the Eaters."

"And the religion," he goes on. "Nine gods, each one an aspect of *the* god. Holiness and wrongness both worshipped. They have hymns, prayers, a theology. And we, the emissaries of the god of wrongness—"

"We're not exterminating them," Michaelson says. "Won't you understand that, Tom? This is all a fantasy of yours. You've been under the influence of drugs, but now we're clearing you out. You'll be clean in a little while. You'll have perspective again."

"A fantasy?" he says bitterly. "A drug dream? I stood out in the prairie and saw you drop pellets. And I watched them die and melt away. I didn't dream that."

"How can we convince you?" Chang asks earnestly. "What will make you believe? Shall we fly over the Eater country with you and show you how many millions there are?"

"But how many millions have already been destroyed?" he demands.

They insist that he is wrong. Ellen tells him again that no one has ever desired to harm the Eaters. "This is a scientific expedition, Tom. We're here to *study* them. It's a violation of all we stand for to injure intelligent life-forms."

"You admit that they're intelligent?"

"Of course. That's never been in doubt."

"Then why drop the pellets?" he asks. "Why slaughter them?"

"None of that has happened, Tom," Ellen says. She takes his hand between her cool palms. "Believe us. Believe us."

He says bitterly, "If you want me to believe you, why don't you do the job properly? Get out the editing machine and go to work on me. You can't simply *talk* me into rejecting the evidence of my own eyes."

"You were under drugs all the time." Michaelson.

"I've never taken drugs! Except for what I ate in the meadow, when I danced—and that came after I had watched the massacre going on for weeks and weeks. Are you saying that it's a retroactive delusion?"

"No, Tom." Schwartz. "You've had this delusion all along. It's part of your therapy, your reconstruct. You came here programmed with it."

"Impossible," he says.

Ellen kisses his fevered forehead. "It was done to reconcile you to mankind, you see. You had this terrible resentment of the displacement of your people in the nineteenth century. You were unable to forgive the industrial society for scattering the Sioux, and you were terribly full of hate. Your therapist thought that if you could be made to participate in an imaginary modern extermination, if you could come to see it as a necessary operation, you'd be purged of your resentment and able to take your place in society as—"

He thrusts her away. "Don't talk idiocy! If you knew the

first thing about reconstruct therapy you'd realize that no reputable therapist could be so shallow. There are no one-to-one correlations in reconstructs. No, don't touch me. Keep away. Keep away."

He will not let them persuade him that this is merely a drug-born dream. It is no fantasy, he tells himself, and it is no therapy. He rises. He goes out. They do not follow him. He takes a copter and seeks his brothers.

Again I dance. The sun is much hotter today. The Eaters are more numerous. Today I wear paint, today I wear feathers. My body shines with my sweat. They dance with me, and they have a frenzy in them that I have never seen before. We pound the trampled meadow with our feet. We clutch for the sun with our hands. We sing, we shout, we cry. We will dance until we fall.

This is no fantasy. These people are real, and they are intelligent, and they are doomed. This I know.

We dance. Despite the doom, we dance.

My great-grandfather comes and dances with us. He too is real. His nose is like a hawk's, not blunt like mine, and he wears the big headdress, and his muscles are like cords under his brown skin. He sings, he shouts, he cries.

Others of my family join us.

We eat the oxygen-plants together. We embrace the Eaters. We know, all of us, what it is to be hunted.

The clouds make music and the wind takes on texture and the sun's warmth has color.

We dance. We dance. Our limbs know no weariness.

The sun grows and fills the whole sky, and I see no Eaters now, only my own people, my father's fathers across the centuries, thousands of gleaming skins, thousands of hawk's noses, and we eat the plants, and we find sharp sticks and thrust them into our flesh, and the sweet blood flows and dries in the blaze of the sun, and we dance, and we dance, and some of us fall from weariness, and we dance, and the prairie is a sea of bobbing head-dresses, an ocean of feathers, and we dance, and my heart makes thunder, and my knees become water, and the sun's fire engulfs me, and I dance, and I fall, and I dance, and I fall, and I fall, and I fall.

Again they find you and bring you back. They give you the cool snout on your arm to take the oxygen-plant drug from your veins, and then they give you something else so you will rest. You rest and you are very calm. Ellen kisses you and you stroke her soft skin, and then the others come in and they talk to you, saying soothing things, but you do not listen, for you are searching for realities. It is not an easy search. It is like falling through many trap doors, looking for the one room whose floor is not hinged. Everything that has happened on this planet is your therapy, you tell yourself, designed to reconcile an embittered aborigine to the white man's conquest; nothing is really being exterminated here. You reject that and fall through and realize that this must be the therapy of your friends; they carry the weight of accumulated centuries of guilts and have come here to shed that load, and you are here to ease them of their burden, to draw their sins into yourself and give them forgiveness. Again you fall through, and see that the Eaters are mere animals who threaten the ecology and must be removed; the culture you imagined for them is your hallucination, kindled out of old churnings. You try to withdraw your objections to this necessary extermination, but you fall through again and discover that there is no extermination except in your mind, which is troubled and disordered by your obsession with the crime against your ancestors, and you sit up, for you wish to apologize to these friends of yours, these innocent scientists whom you have called murderers. And you fall through.